TWO FOR TEA

WELCOME TO AZATHÈ

USA TODAY BESTSELLING AUTHOR

CM NASCOSTA

MEDUÀS
EDITORIALE

MEDUÁS
EDITORIALE

CONTENTS

Author's Note

This is the unhorniest book I've ever written — and that's okay.

Because sometimes life is about more than the sexy monster next door — it's about pulling yourself back up from the deepest depths, showing yourself the same grace you extend to others, and allowing your heart time to heal. Also, that matching blacks that did not come off the same dye lot is an underrated life skill I wish more people had. This book might not be for you, and that's okay too.

Harper is a bi demisexual (but still very sexual) FMC. Azathé is a non-binary (and very non-human) MC. The journey through healing looks different for everyone, but the pain of loss in universal, regardless of even species. I tried hard to make sure they were not cardboard cutouts, and I hope you find their story to be one with which you can relate, even if you are not an incorporeal shadow creature.

At this point in the game, if you are not following along with ALL of the Cambric Creek stories, I no longer know if "can be enjoyed as a standalone" is accurate. It CAN be, but the fullest appreciation will come with having read the other books in my Cambric Creek universe to this point. Special thanks to A.Bash for providing Holt with such an I-can't-believe-this-is-real canvas.

For Gosia ♥

+ · · · + · · · + · · · + · · · + · · · + · · · +

Content Advisories:

Depression and grief, and lots of it. Parental Death. Suicidal ideation. Mentions of off-page dubcon. Use of holistic medicine — Ladybug is not a doctor and neither am I, so please don't use this book as an instructional manual for self medication.

✦ · · ✦ · · ✦ · · ✦ · · ✦ · · ✦ · · ✦ · · ✦

If you or someone you love is in crisis, help is a single call/text away:

Call or text 988 in the United States

https://findahelpline.com/

Chapter 1

"I want the cabinet on *this* wall, I think . . . and the table placed just in front of it. I want this workspace to be absolutely perfect. Hmm . . . no, a bit more to the left."

The movers shrugged, shifting the table a few negligible centimeters as her mother squinted, surveying the landscape of the room as if she were an explorer looking out from the summit of Mount Everest for the very first time after a brutal ascent, finding the view to be somewhat lacking.

"Ilea, can we make sure none of the crystals sustained any damage during the move? Let's catalog everything, please. I don't want to find out that the jasper points are chipped six months from now when my moving warranty is only good for the next week. Just a bit more to the left, now . . . perfect, right there. Everything is perfect."

Perfect. Everything had to be *perfect* at all times. Every thing at every moment of every waking hour of the day. Perfection was the only state her mother accepted, from her wardrobe to her home to her daughters. Harper hung back, not wanting to mar the *perfect* landscape of her mother's new workroom with her distinct *im*perfection. Unfortunately, her attempt to escape notice was in vain.

"Harper, darling, why don't you find another one of the movers and direct them on where to put all of your things. Although it will be a wonder if they can even fit the furniture through the door."

"I'm sure the door is a normal door, mother. Don't they have building codes?"

Her mother tutted, turning her attention back once more to the cabinet and the precise placement of the table before it.

"Ilea, let's make sure we have room to leave the upper shelf open for display. Pru Hevisham mentioned something about the new coven taking turns with hosting duties."

The very notion of entertaining had her mother practically bouncing on her toes in excitement. Harper swallowed hard, hoping her face didn't betray the dread she felt at the mere thought of having to be *perfect* and on display for an entire day under her mother's watchful eye. *Sisters, let me be the first to introduce you all to my eldest daughter, the failure.*

"I've no idea what their rotation looks like, but I'm hoping we can be added to it as soon as possible. Who knows, we might be hosting a welcoming tea! Let's make sure everything is set up flawlessly *now*. Set it and forget it."

A lie, for her mother never forgot a thing and would fuss and tinker with every detail until every speck of the room, down to the last dust mote, had passed muster.

"Of course," Ilea agreed, making a show of jotting something down on their tablet face. "We may as well take care of it now. Work smarter, not harder."

Harper was certain if she rolled her eyes any harder, they would rotate right out of her head and go spinning across the floor, lost to the unpacking detritus forever. *Perfection, always perfection. Work smarter, not harder. Keep it simple, stupid. A goal without a plan is just a wish without directions.* Her mother was full of the sort of platitudes one might find on a motivational poster at one's therapist's office, or else, the nuggets of wisdom imparted by the daytime manager of a quick service restaurant to their team in a meeting full of chants and hand clapping. She would need to find a new therapist here, eventually, and fortunately, her days of fast food service were behind her, leaving her little appreciation for her mother's bon mots.

"I can't imagine garden sheds have the same standards as an ordinary household door."

Harper jumped when she realized the jab was directed at her, the conversation resuming without warning. Ilea was poisonous in every form. The familiar had sunk into the role of personal assistant with gusto, an ever-present tablet and stylus in hand, trailing after Harper's mother constantly, an inescapable presence and the bane of her miserable existence since moving back home.

"It's hardly going to be big enough for you to even turn around in there, you know. I still don't understand why you don't just take one of the rooms upstairs and move your—"

Her mother was once again facing the cabinet as she spoke, providing the perfect opportunity for Harper to drift out of the room.

As much as she didn't like being ordered around as if she were a child, checking in on her things was not a bad idea. The movers had, to her knowledge, already delivered her carefully labeled belongings, but it was worth dou-ble-checking, especially if it got her out of her mother's bubble of awareness.

The carriage house was connected to the main house by a gravel driveway, sitting back some twenty or thirty yards, shaded by a line of enormous elms and maple trees. It was hardly a garden shed. Technically, it wasn't even a carriage house at all, even though that was how the real estate agent had suggested listing it. There was no open ground floor area, nothing large enough or wide enough for a carriage or vehicle to pass through, no stable where there may have once been horses.

It was a cottage, she decided. A tiny cottage just big enough for her, its back door leading to a winding flagstone path that led to the back garden, to the lilac grove and pink honeysuckle, moon flowers and hellebore and showy white datura, their heraldic trumpets only opening beneath the moon. It was a perfect witch's cottage, and the only thing that could have possibly made it better was for it to have a different address entirely, perhaps across town in the middle of the actual woods. Instead, it was less than one hundred feet from her mother's back door, a fact which dampened her enthusiasm for her new living quarters greatly. *Well, that and you're hardly a witch. You may as well just call it a carriage house, after all.*

The movers had indeed already done their work, she was relieved to see. All of her things, every box from her apartment, the few pieces of furniture she kept, everything had been painstakingly labeled — *CARRIAGE HOUSE ~ HARPER* — and she was relieved to see doing so had paid off. What the movers had *not* done, however, was actually move any of the furniture into any of the designated rooms. Not that her new abode could boast many of those.

A tiny, compact kitchen just off the living room, a single bedroom, a miniature bathroom, and a room that was having an identity crisis — too small to be a proper bedroom, too large to be a linen closet, it seemed utterly without purpose to her, with a tiny, diamond-shaped window near the top of the wallpapered wall. Perhaps, she thought, she might turn it into a small reading nook. She could line the two sidewalls in shelves and wedge an armchair beneath the odd little window. *Perfect. And then you never need to leave.*

Despite the proximity to her mother and her own questionable claim to witchiness, the cottage was perfect. She envisioned it in autumn — a carpet of crimson leaves from the overhead maples carpeting the walkway, a miniature hay bale set outside the front door holding a collection of decorative gourds, with a festive jack-o-lantern beside it. In spring, the lilacs would be in bloom, perfuming the air, and she would put in flower boxes on the two small front windows. In the summer, she would charge spring water and crystals beneath the full moon in the secluded backyard, disrobing and performing the ancient rites on her own, no catty coven necessary.

The movers had left her furniture clustered in the living room — a loveseat that had been a floor model and purchased at half cost, two cheap pressed-wood bookshelves with unpronounceable-to-her-eyes Scandinavian names, a wingback chair, and her bed. Her undersized kitchen table had been disassembled, and at first, she didn't quite realize that the round, wooden table all her boxes were stacked upon was not the one she had moved with. It was too heavy, too sturdy, and she realized it must've been left in the cottage when the house was emptied after her grandmother's death.

Deciding she could move her meager furniture on her own and that doing a bit of lugging was a preferable scenario to having one of the movers invading her space once more, Harper pushed up the sleeves of her black dress.

The bed was easy enough to slide across the floor once she positioned the moving skates she'd had in one of the boxes beneath each leg, and she wondered, as she carefully walked her mattress down the hallway, one slow step at a time, if this was how the ancients had constructed the standing stone circles she'd visited on a trip to Europe, years earlier.

She would need to buy a storage shelf for the small kitchen, she realized once all of the boxes holding her utensils and gadgets and pantry items had been moved to the small galley space. She had loved cooking once and had amassed an array of tools that had been long neglected. *Maybe you can start cooking again, you can even take a class. Mom said this place has tons of programs through the community center. Who knows, you might decide to make potion brewer your designation.*

A scuffling sound in her front door interrupted her musing, bringing her head up sharply. Harper crossed the small room in a few steps, assuming one of the movers had left a box on

11

the small stoop. Instead, she found Ilea's lithe body stretched against the doorframe, dropping quickly when it opened and nearly stumbling backward. Her eyes narrowed instantly, feeling defensive.

Her mother's poisonous familiar only took a moment to recover from their momentary inelegance, nose raising as they took her in. "Ah, Harper. You *did* manage to find your way over. We weren't sure."

Her hand tightened around the door. *Fucking Ilea.* "You weren't sure if I would find my way fifty feet up the driveway? Well, I'm thrilled to burst your bubble, but it was a pretty straight shot. No trouble at all."

Their face was already screwed up in its familiar sour lemon pucker, tightening further at her words. "Be that as it may, your mother thinks one or two of her boxes may have been moved into your little shack here. I'm just going to check for —"

They made a move to step through the doorway, but Harper refused to budge, blocking entry to her new home. *Not today, Satan. Not today.* "They didn't. I've already gone through all the boxes the movers brought in and sorted them into the right rooms. They're all mine."

"I think I'd feel better checking for myself. No offense, darling, but you're not exactly known for your thorough workmanship."

"I said I've already checked through the boxes." Her voice was sharp, her feet planted firmly. *They're going to need to knock you down and force their way in*. She would double-check as soon as Ilea had left, but there was no way she was allowing the familiar into her home. They would taint it with their very presence.

The cat had resented and despised her from the moment she'd been born. Ilea had been with her mother since she was a teen, a status symbol in the world of hereditary witchcraft. Taking the shape of a fluffy, silver point persian cat, they hovered at her mother's side in the dozen framed photos that adorned the sitting room wall in her grandmother's house. Ilea had gone with her to school, to the Collegium, moving away from Cambric Creek after she met and married Harper's father, himself the son of a witch. Fully entrenched and completely comfortable . . . until Harper was born.

Harper didn't know the specifics. Only that Ilea fast depleted their welcome, once Harper had arrived, a squalling bundle who came between witch and familiar. Ilea had pressured her mother, encouraging her to turn her attention away from her newborn daughter, back to her craft, until Harper's father had put his foot down, deciding his leniency for the cat in their home had reached its end. Ilea had returned to Harper's grandmother's house, being given a choice to either wait out infancy or return to the Coalition of

Magical Imps for a new placement. *And they've hated you for it ever since.*

Ilea and her mother had fallen into a pattern of long-distance study and assistance once Harper was a toddler, coming to stay with them for two-week stretches of time every few months, stretches that gradually lengthened, a pattern that lasted seven long years until Morgan was born, sealing the cat out of their house for good. *Until now.* Harper had always been the target of their ire, as if she had collaborated with mystic forces in the womb to force Ilea from their home and her mother's side.

"If it turns out I'm wrong, I'll bring it over later. And if my mother needs something right this second, she can come over and get it herself." *What are you doing sniffing around my doorway, anyway?*

Ilea snickered as they turned from the doorway after stiffening for the space of a heartbeat. "*If.* Harper," they drawled her name in a mocking manner, clicking their tongue. "Sweetie, we all know there's no if about it. *If* you're wrong."

Her insides clenched against whatever venomous words were about to come dripping off the cat's barbed tongue. Rationally, she knew she shouldn't take anything Ilea said to heart, but rationality was in short supply these days, and the lizard who lurked in the back of her brain loved latching on any and all outside negativity, feeding it to the black hole in her chest.

"Failing at things is practically second nature for you now, sugarplum. You being wrong is a given."

She watched them saunter back up the gravel drive, an echoing gong seeming to come from the empty place inside of her. She knew Ilea was hateful and cruel . . . But that didn't mean they were wrong. A hateful truth wasn't any less true. *Fucking Ilea*.

She stepped back into her little cottage after locking the door behind her, surveying the mess in the kitchen with fresh, wearier eyes. *You don't need a shelf. You need to get rid of all this stuff. You haven't cooked a real meal in almost a year. You don't need to make room for another abandoned hobby. You need to sell this shit at whatever secondhand store will take it because, oh yeah, you flunked out of school, and you don't have a job.*

The chastisement came out of nowhere, and Harper sagged, defeated. The voice in her head had grown steadily louder over the course of the year, the most wretched year of her life, drowning out her other thoughts until she wasn't sure where it ended, and she began.

In any case, she thought heavily, it was probably right. Cooking had been fun once, but the thought of going through the motions, the work of putting together a meal for one, left her exhausted. *For that matter, you can probably get rid of most of this crap. Abandoned hobbies, projects you started and never finished, a waste of space. Why bother unpacking it? As a reminder that you're incapable of finishing something you start? Are these your emotional support crochet supplies? You've never even finished a scarf.*

The cottage windows did not yet possess any curtains, and she was forced to turn the loveseat around, its back facing the front door, leaving her free to curl up invisibly. There were only two times when the voice could not reach her — when she was lost in a book and when she was asleep. Her books were still packed away, and her enthusiasm for turning the cozy space into a real home had vanished.

It was self-care to sleep when she was tired, she told herself, tucking her knees to her chest as she lay against the loveseat's cushions. She was exhausted and heavy and tired of *feeling*, and escaping the voice in her head seemed more important than unpacking the boxes of evidence of her *imperfection* just then. Closing her eyes, Harper let the world fall away until her conscious mind was silenced at last.

Chapter 2

She hadn't realized, at least not until that past year, that there was a right way to grieve.

Grief, Harper had always assumed, was a personal thing. That the crushing agony of loss lessened with time, as everyone claimed it did — that she would be overwhelmed with sadness until the day she simply wasn't. Most importantly, everyone around her would either be feeling similarly or, at the very least, understanding and patient.

The past year and a half had been instructional in showing her just how mistaken she was. There was, she had learned, in fact, a wrong way to grieve. There was good grief, and there was bad grief, and it was likely a surprise to absolutely no one that she had somehow gotten tangled up in the latter.

Good grief was pretty and sympathetic, organized and pragmatic, and most importantly, it was finite. Good grief was her mother's brave face at the funeral, poised and somber in her black sheath dress and dark glasses, graciously welcoming the endless line of people who had come to pay their respects. It was the way her mother and Ilea had descended upon the closet in the master bedroom a month later to strip half of it bare, filling bags for the donation pile, and then again when they had downsized the furniture as the one-year anniversary loomed, preparations made to sell the house Harper and her sister had grown up in, where her father's memory lived in every room, lingered in every doorway and corner, where she was positive she was still able to hear the echo of his laughter across the kitchen.

It was just a house, her mother had said. *Too much space with the girls leaving the nest. Too much property to look after on your own. You have enough on your plate. Best to downsize, think of the future.* Extended family and well-wishers were quick to agree that the house was merely a house.

It was just a house, Harper had agreed in a stupor — just a wooden box, no different from any of the other wooden boxes on the tree-lined street, if they were all stripped down to their studs. The tree-lined street where she and her sister had learned to ride bikes, where she'd taken the first photograph she'd ever entered into a contest — the full moon ringed in a crimson halo through the sparsely-leaved branches of the ancient oak tree in the front yard. And it wasn't even a house she had lived in for several years, despite still having a bedroom full of belongings there. Belongings and memories in the wood smoke smell of the forge drifting upwards to the house every afternoon, the comforting smell of her father and *home*.

It was just a house, she had reminded herself the first time she'd walked into it to find it empty, not a stick of furniture left. Every little sound echoed noisily across the hardwood floors in the empty rooms, drowning out the echo of memories and laughter and happiness. *It was just a house* as she pulled away from it for the last time.

Bad grief was driving from the empty house that was no longer their home straight to the liquor store. She'd wound up at the playground where she and her sister had played every afternoon as children, where their father had pulled them in the wagon until she was too big, and then she walked beside him, leaving Morgan in the wagon with her doll.

She'd sat at the top of the monkey bars — the same ones she'd fallen off when she was ten, splitting open her lip, the same ones her father had lifted her back onto just a few weeks after her fall, encouraging her not to be afraid to try again — polishing off the bottle she'd purchased, her shoulders shaking with the force of her sobs. She had screamed like a feral animal, like the banshees from whom they were descended until her throat was hoarse and her bottle empty.

Bad grief was waking in the middle of the night in the bed of a stranger, with no idea who he was or how she'd wound up there. She would collect her tights from the floor, when she could find them, a swift look in the nearest mirror showing her the reflection of a gaunt wraith, smeared black eyeliner and mascara melting into the deep shadows beneath her red-rimmed eyes, giving her a raccoon-like appearance, and she would turn away, frightened by the dead-eyed foreigner in the mirror.

Bad grief was missing lectures and labs, several days' worth of missed classes a week. Absences followed by unfocused apathy when she did manage to be present as if her meat suit had navigated its way across the Collegium's campus, but her consciousness was still cocooned in bed, unable to find the will or energy to rouse itself.

A witch's education was different from the standard university experience. She'd acquired a fine arts degree at the neighboring state school, attending classes at the Collegium several days a week throughout undergrad for core competencies, but her formal education in witchcraft did not truly begin until her undergraduate studies were complete. A gap year or two, either traveling or working and then choosing the specialty to which she would devote herself and her craft, not becoming a fully accredited member of the coven for at least another decade, once she'd proven herself adept in her field.

That she'd spent her gap year burying the only parent who'd ever understood her seemed inconsequential to the planned schedule of events.

The witch assigned as her counselor had sat across the desk at the end of the term with a frown, looking over Harper's abysmal results. "Fortunately, you are still early in your path," the witch had told her with a kind smile, as if she were doing Harper a favor by telling her she was expelled. "And that is a fortuitous thing. You haven't even declared a discipline yet. There's plenty of time to come back, once . . . well, once you're able to handle the responsibility of full-time studies again. Self-care is not something you ought to be ignoring right now, Ms. Hollingsworth. A witch unable to care for her own well-being will never be able to provide service to her community or coven. I hope you seek the help you need. You'll need to retake the entry exams, of course, but the Collegium's doors will be open to you, once you're fit to return."

Bad grief was sitting numbly before the counselor witch, silent as her invitation to return to school the following term was rescinded, not finding her voice until she was standing before the frozen case at the mini-mart off campus. Her voice had come back to her in the form of noisy sobs, shuddering out in between the orange creamsicles and crinkle-cut fries, snot and drool and red-splotched skin, barely able to hold herself up.

The handful of other shoppers had circled her warily, an employee appearing at her elbow to ask if she was alright. She'd been unable to answer, the noises coming out of her sounding more like a wounded animal than a witch. Harper had attempted to bat off his hand around her elbow, winding up sliding to the floor. Another employee had appeared, each of them gripping her beneath her armpits, and she'd not had the energy to fight. They deposited her outside of the mini-mart's door, leaning her against the wall like a sack of garbage, until the police cruiser had shown up and her sobs began anew.

Bad grief was sitting in the back of the police car, listening as the responding officers debated bringing her to the hospital or simply bringing her home.

"P-please just bring me home. I don't want to go to the hospital. I swear I'm not crazy, okay? I just . . . my father died and I'm not going back to school and I just . . . please bring me home. I'm sorry for causing any trouble."

The officers had softened, the one behind the wheel asking for her address while the eyebrows belonging to the woman in the passenger seat drew together as she met Harper's eye in the rearview mirror.

"Hey," the woman said as she deposited Harper on her stoop after they rolled into the parking lot of her small off-campus apartment building. "*Crazy* doesn't mean anything, okay? That word doesn't have any meaning. We all need help sometimes. A few days of inpatient might do you some good. And all *that* means is you need a bit of help right now, got it? Is there someone you can call?"

She had mumbled that she would be contacting her mother, promising the police officers she would do so as soon as she was inside, although it was several hours before she had composed herself sufficiently to make the call home. *Home. Another word that doesn't have any meaning.*

Bad grief was eating ice cream for breakfast. Her mother had called out the very behavior months earlier, but her mother wasn't there just then, and there was no one at all around to see as she pulled a pint of cappuccino mocha chip from the freezer, dropping to the sofa with a teaspoon. Bad grief was an endless rotation of bad reality television and online shopping, taking the place of fresh air, exercise, and gainful employment. Bad grief was sleeping until two p.m. each day, even though she was positive sleep counted as self-care.

But more than anything else, the most significant difference between good grief and bad was that bad grief was as endless as the ocean, with no respite or relief in sight.

She was bobbing on the waves with no hope of rescue and nothing but the voice in her head and the gaping hole in her chest for company, and Harper was beginning to wonder if she ought to simply succumb to the undertow.

She didn't know if all the people who somehow managed to perform good grief, people like her mother, were still shredded on the inside. She didn't know if they were still consumed with emptiness and longing for the way things used to be, or if they had all somehow filled in the hole left in their heart with friends and partners and community activism and social clubs. *Maybe everyone is miserable all the time, and you're just the only one who's shit at hiding it.*

+·+·+·+·+·+·+·+·+·+

OOTD: Bat-print leggings. Grey t-shirt with Nietzsche quote about suffering. Overwhelming sense of futility. Fuzzy socks with pumpkins, because it's never too early to be thinking about Fall.

The buzz of her phone distracted her from her laptop screen for a moment, a text from her younger sister.

Mom said make sure you're dressed and ready by noon.

Harper rolled her eyes. Her mother had gotten her wish, at least partially. A handful of witches from the coven were coming by that afternoon for tea, a two p.m. affair, hardly necessitating her fidgeting in her grandmother's dining room for two hours.

It's not like Morgan is going to be ready by then either. She and her seventeen-year-old sister were close enough, but still being in high school gave her sister something to fixate on, gave her focus and drive.

She's going to leave for the Collegium and university and you're going to be stuck here with mom and Ilea forever. Wrinkling her nose at the thought, she snuggled into the corner of the sofa with her ice cream and laptop. It had been several months since she'd left the Collegium with the order to do exactly that. Now the summer waned and witches would soon be returning to those echoing, hallowed halls. She'd not be among them. She wasn't ready, still as unfocused and apathetic as she had been that day in the counselor's office. She needed to give herself time to rest and heal, to stay in bed as long as her body needed and eat all the cappuccino mocha chip ice cream she wanted, and if her mother ever wanted her to rejoin polite society, Harper thought, her self-care should be the priority.

Holding her spoon in her mouth, she tapped open a familiar page. She had discovered an occult shop in the neighboring city that did an online auction every week on one of their social media accounts. The hypnotic voice of the woman who ran the auction was second only to the well-shaped hands of the man who held and placed the items, drawing the viewer's eye with his long, lacquered black claws.

She had never purchased anything from the shop, possessing neither the space nor the money to start collecting haunted pocket watches and antique mortuary equipment, but her little goth heart loved watching the auctions each week, and she discovered that by watching the recording the afternoon following the live event, she could enjoy the spooky objects, the man's hands, the woman's voice, all while protecting her bank balance.

"A poison ring from 1763, taken from the excavations of a Tuscan Villa. Trace amounts of powdered belladonna are still embedded in the engraving on the inside of the hinged lid. The home this was taken from belonged to a witch of great renown, and it is likely this ring helped her keep her place as a confidant to local politicians. Let's get the bidding started, shall we?"

She had just swallowed a spoonful of her ice cream when a sharp rapping against the glass pane of her front door merely made her choke. Morgan was the only one who slapped on doors with an open palm, having learned in childhood that she was able to create more of a racket, and the more noise she made, the faster she got her way. Harper struggled to push herself from her ass groove in the corner of the sofa, legs tangled in her blanket, staggering the few paces across the room to the door.

"Holy shit, stop that right this instant. What is wrong with you?"

Her younger sister didn't bother answering, pushing past Harper and crossing to the sofa. Morgan dropped into her ass groove, picking up the ice cream.

"I forgot you always liked coffee ice cream. Mom is on a low-fat everything kick right now, all we have in the house is vanilla made with skim milk and it tastes like the dessert equivalent of forgetting why you walked into the room. Or like, you know how it feels when you have to drop something off at the post office and you get there and it turns out to be some human holiday and everything is closed? That's how that ice cream tastes. *This* shit, however, is delicious. I have to remember you have it."

"You are such a mooch," Harper laughed, retrieving a second teaspoon from the kitchen before dropping to the sofa beside her sister. Morgan made no protest when she tapped her auction back on, and they watched in companionable silence as an alligator skull was shown, followed by an Odd Fellows death mask.

"This guy has sexy hands. Is he ever on camera?"

She shook her head, spooning up a scoop full of the ice cream. "He's not. Unfortunately. He doesn't talk either, only the woman."

Morgan snorted. "That's a waste. Maybe he has a really obnoxious voice. Wait, I like that ring. How much is it?"

"It's an auction. It's not just for sale with the price, you have to bid on it."

"Well, bid on it! Wait, does it show you how much it's going for?"

Harper threw up her hands. "It's not a live auction! This is from yesterday evening."

Morgan turned to her in disgust. "What is the point in watching an auction that's already over? You can't bid on anything? This is like watching someone else's wedding on YouTube."

She laughed in outrage, snatching the ice cream back from her sister. "You know what, get out. I don't have to take this kind of abuse in my own home."

Morgan pushed to her feet, using Harper's forehead for leverage, making her yelp in laughter.

"Fine, but you have to come with me. That's why I came over in the first place. Mom wants you to get ready and come up to the house so that we are all ready. She probably wants to prep us on acceptable conversation topics."

Harper groaned, dropping her head back against the sofa. "Why? Her little party isn't for another three hours."

"Probably because she's worried you're going to fall asleep and come staggering over in your pajamas." Morgan shrugged.

"Come on, I did that like, one time!"

"It's been more like three times, actually," her sister shot back, shaking her head. "One of them being my birthday dinner, now that you mention it."

Harper averted her eyes. When she was asleep, she was free from the picking little voice in her head, and it was easier to sleep than it was to face her uncertain future and well-documented imperfection.

"Harper . . . will you please do me a favor?"

She glanced up at her sister's more serious tone. *Please don't ask me to be better. Please don't ask me to snap out of it. If I could do that, don't you think I would have already?* Morgan sucked in a breath between her teeth before continuing.

"Look, I'm not any happier about moving than you. Do you really think I wanted to leave all my friends junior year? It sucks, and it's just one more thing that has sucked in the past two years. But it is what it is, Harper. Promise me you're going to try here? I'm not going to be here in two years to bang on the door and make you get out of bed. It's bad enough that we lost Dad, but now I feel like I'm losing my sister too."

A lump of shame had formed in her throat, blocking her airway and making it impossible to breathe. Her sister was right, of course. She was failing Morgan just like she had failed at everything else.

"Like, it's bad enough that the independent study program starts in fucking *July*. I shouldn't be in school this early. That should be illegal. But there's this guy on the lacrosse team in my independent study. I think he's a werewolf. Or maybe a shifter? Whatever, but like, every time he walks in the room, I can hear the voice from that one meme. 'I *know* his dick is big, I know it is.'"

She almost choked. The lump of shame was shoved aside, her strangled laughter escaping in its place as Morgan continued.

"And I hate that I don't have you to talk to about that. Because, like, I think about it all the time. *All* the time. So I'm just saying, please don't make me lose you too. Promise me you're going to get up and leave the house every day, even if it's just to take a walk. The Vitamin D will do you good. You need to get out of your head, and getting up is the first step, I'm pretty sure. Maybe you should get a cat or something. Oh, I know! You can have Ilea!"

"Out," Harper ordered, pointing at the door. "I was with you until that point. Give me, like, fifteen minutes to get dressed, and I'll be over. I promise . . . About everything," she added, averting her eyes once more.

It was, Harper knew from previous promises to herself that she was going to magically get better, a tall order her sister was asking. *Still*, she thought, pushing to her feet, *you don't need Mom to have one more thing to bitch about. And Ilea doesn't need any more ammunition*. She would be on time to her mother's tea, she decided, pulling out one of her favorite dresses. *The patent Mary Janes. The velvet choker. You can do this. Do it for Morgan, at least for today. Then you can go back to bed.*

Her sister, she decided a few hours later, trying to be as invisible as possible amidst the assembled gossiping witches, was right. She needed to start getting up every single day and getting out of the house. Otherwise, she was going to be pressed into service, studying alongside her mother and Ilea, and Harper would rather chew glass.

"You haven't yet chosen a designation, dear?"

She realized belatedly that the question was directed at her, the speaker a middle-aged woman with a sleek blonde bob, as neat and prim as the other four women who sat around the table. Several of them had their own daughters in tow, mirror images of their mothers, and she noticed, perhaps clearly for the very first time, just how much she stuck out, even in her own family.

She and her sister had both favored their father in looks — pale complexions and dark hair, and she had never grown out of her goth phase, much to her mother's chagrin. The three young women around the table varied in age, between her and Morgan, and they all looked as if they had stepped from the pages of an advertisement for a week-long summer concert festival. Floral dresses, elegant jewel tones, trendy if not conservative cuts. Harper glanced surreptitiously down at her own dress — a frothy chiffon confection with puffed sleeves and a crystal pleated skirt — all in jet black, matching her jet black hair, her jet black nails, her winged eyeliner and mascara. She was just as appropriately dressed as anyone else at the table, she rationalized. She had simply chosen a more basic color palette. *And what's wrong with that?*

"N-no, I haven't. Still, um, weighing my options."

The question was asked as if she had not yet started her practical study at the Collegium, as if she were still in her gap year. She wondered if that was the story her mother had told them, deciding that the answer was likely yes. Her mother had been eager to reconnect with her old coven friends, witches she had known since she was a teenager. *She probably told them you haven't gone back to school yet. She doesn't want them to know about Harper, the failure.*

After all, no one knew her in Cambric Creek other than her family and Ilea. No one knew about the missed classes and subsequent expulsion from the program, no one here had been present to bear witness to her mini-mart break-down. Her sister was right. She could start fresh air. Become an entirely new person, if she wanted.

"I am so thrilled to have such a spacious work area that doesn't have to pull double duty as the family kitchen," her mother trilled. "I've already told Ilea that Harper and I are going to be like two little star pupils starting next week. We're going to go through every discipline for refresher work, it'll be good for both of us. And it will help you make your decision, darling." A beatific smile, one Harper met with a grimace. *Glass. We're gonna chew it.*

"Tara, we can't wait for you and the girls to meet Evelyn. She's so dynamic! The coven has changed so much. Nothing at all like what you remember."

"The one thing I *will* say, though," another witch piped up, her eyes casting about as if to ensure there were no sudden eavesdroppers in the room, "Authricia placed such emphasis on the younger girls, and I do miss that. Our Kennedy is taking her junior placements right now, and I don't feel she has the same foundation we all benefited from."

There was a hum of agreement from two of the other women, her mother raising an eyebrow as Harper took it all in.

"Montgomerie is finishing her practicum studies right now," another hushed voice, all the women in attendance leaning forward slightly in their chairs. "She lives out west, and I'm just not sure if the things she's being taught at the school there are going to align very well with the coven's new principles." Another one of those fast glances around as if there might be someone hovering over the group listening in. "Some of the potion requirements Evelyn has are certainly controversial in certain circles."

Murmurs and mutters, and suddenly, no one in the room was willing to meet the eye of the witch beside her.

"But-but like I said, she is so *dynamic*! She's brought about a dramatic change; she really put her mark on the coven here. We're so excited to have you back!"

+·····+·····+·····+·····+

"What do you suppose all that meant?"

Her mother's voice was hushed. The house was empty and echoing once more, the witches departed. Morgan was engrossed with something on her phone, not paying any attention to the way their mother hovered in the doorway of the foyer, peeking out the sidelights as her tea guests pulled away.

Ilea shrugged. "It means this coven finally has a high crone unafraid of putting our ambitions ahead of the petty bickering and egos in this community. Authricia was a fine witch, but she was the werewolves' puppet. You'll love Evelyn."

Harper frowned. She was disinclined to agree with Ilea on anything, which made their pronouncement of this high witch being one they would all love highly unlikely. Their words felt cryptic, and even though she didn't know the first thing about the witches in this neighborhood, didn't know anything about the neighborhood itself, and wasn't sure if she could even be considered one of them, Harper was sure a coven actively working against the needs and wants of its community seemed entirely contrary to everything she had been taught in school.

There is no way you're studying with Ilea. You can just move to Bridgeton and live as a normal human. Maybe get a job at the paper, or in a coffee shop, or whoever will hire you, it's not like you can do anything. Morgan is right. You need to get up and get out of the fucking house. Don't give them the opportunity to rope you into whatever mom is planning. She would get up the following morning after her sister left for school, she decided. The car engine always woke her up, and most days she went right back to bed, but that was going to change. *Pack your books and your laptop. Go somewhere and read. Just get out of the house and remove yourself as a target.*

She would much rather stay home, Harper thought, once she was snuggled back into the ass groove on her loveseat, wrapped in her blanket with her laptop on her knees, cappuccino mocha chip pint beside her. She would rather stay in bed, sleeping away the reminder that other witches her age would be rising to attend class, preparing for their futures . . . But leaving the house was preferable to whatever her mother had planned, and there was no way around it.

Chapter 3

OTD: The silk blend knee socks and stacked platform loafers. The pleated skirt dress with the Peter Pan collar. The double stitched blazer.

She nodded decisively in the mirror as she readied herself, finishing her look with a black lip stain. Just because she wasn't heading back to class with her contemporaries didn't mean she couldn't look the part. Harper slipped out the door, determined to make herself scarce.

It did not take long to realize she was a stranger to Cambric Creek in more ways than one, regardless of the time she may have spent here in her youth. The late summer sky was a wash of white-dotted blue, and although the sun was shining, a breeze kept the tree branches moving, a perfect day to leave the house . . . and promptly go indoors, someplace else. Getting out of the house was the main imperative. Harper decided she was library-bound, craving nothing more than a quiet place where she could curl up and read her book, quieting her mind, uninterrupted.

Harper set off on foot, tentatively knowing from her cursory explorations of the map on her cell phone that she could pick up a bus that passed through Cambric Creek's downtown area. Her family's home was at the edge of an area known as Oldetowne, and during her twilight meanderings, she had discovered that while the house was grand to her and had seemed cavernous when she was a child, it paled in comparison to the stately properties owned by some of their neighbors just a few blocks in.

There was one such residence at the end of Magnolia Street that had made her jaw drop open, the first time she passed. Grey stone, four stories high from what she was able to tell, iron cresting at the roof line, leaded windows winking, the house had been at once magnificent and hideous. It was set back from the road, the long drive buffeted by snarling stone figures and a wrought iron gate. Harper wasn't sure how long she had stood there gaping at the stone edifice, but her skin had begun to prickle, feeling eyes on her, watching her stare at the house. The Victorian beside it, an ornately designed Queen Anne, had a shadow in one of the upper windows, one that shifted as she began to walk again, and Harper would hurry up the sidewalk, away from the homes, the feeling of observance not passing until she had rounded the corner.

The bus, when it arrived, turned out not to be a bus at all, but an old-fashioned open-air trolley, and Harper wondered if she looked as ridiculous as she felt, swinging her bat wing backpack over her shoulder as she climbed aboard, taking her seat behind two gossiping goblins in pastel activewear. She watched as a trio of sleek young women boarded at the stop on the corner opposite a long line of condominiums, selkies, she guessed, based on the identical sable-colored fur coats draped over their shoulders. *They're probably students at the school. You should enroll, take some classes and get an English Lit degree. You can move to Bridgeton and be a teacher and pretend you've never even heard of witchcraft.*

"Excuse me," she leaned over the seat slightly at the first break in the goblin's conversation, as the shops of Main Street neared, "this is the stop for the library, right?"

One of the petite, green-skinned women turned, giving Harper a pitying smile. "It is, but I'm afraid it's still closed for renovation."

Dammit. She should have checked the website. Harper's shoulders slumped, as the other goblin continued.

"The building had a pipe break at its main and there was a major flooding issue. I understand it was a lot of damage, but it seems like it's taking for*ever*. It's been weeks! The high school students are able to use the campus library, but what are the little ones supposed to do? Storytime has been moved to the community center, but it's not the same. We keep hearing it'll be reopening at the end of the month, but you know how that goes."

"I wouldn't doubt it," the first goblin cut in, standing as the trolley slowed. "Jack's grandson goes to story time, and you know how *that* goes."

The goblin women laughed, exiting the trolley as Harper scrambled to scoop up her belongings, deciding she might be able to find a sleepy little coffee shop to hide in amidst the downtown landscape.

She found the coffee shop with little trouble, not that she stayed long enough to even place an order. The Black Sheep Beanery was a cacophony of sound — students, office dwellers, construction workers, and everyone in between. 'Sleepy' was not a description it could boast unless she planned on returning in the middle of the night, and even then she wasn't willing to count on it.

The town she'd grown up in had its fair mix of goblins and trolls, but Harper had never before been surrounded by folks of so many different species the way she was at that moment.

"For God's sake, Byron, do you ever just stop and think before opening your mouth?!"

She listened as the vampire in front of her in line berated someone on the phone, overheard a snippet of conversation from the two activewear-clad goblins in line behind her — not the same two from the trolley, she noted after a swift glance over her shoulder, and as she watched, a broad-shouldered man in an immaculately tailored suit breezed through the doors, circumventing the long line of patrons, moving to the opposite side of the counter from the pick-up area. He gave the ewe-faced woman behind the counter a blinding white smile as two drinks were placed in front of him by the ram manning the espresso machine. Harper shook her head as the man was checked out on a handheld device, oblivious to the two dozen people he'd cut.

"You leave today?" the ram asked, as the man tapped his credit card to the handheld checkout, answering in the affirmative. "We'll be looking for you in the paper. Give 'em hell."

"Oh, I plan on it," the big man said with another dazzling smile, leaving as quickly as he'd arrived.

A throng of college-age students and chattering mothers pushing strollers were taking up a not-insignificant portion of the dining area, and Harper realized there would be no quiet nook to disappear into, not here. Her desire for caffeine wasn't as strong as her desperate need to lose herself for a bit, and while the Black Sheep Beanery might deliver on one half of that equation, the second, more important half was likely an impossibility with so much noise and commotion.

Leaving her place in the line, she found herself back on the sidewalk.

She had a hard time remembering any specifics of the town from her childhood, for visits to her grandmother rarely necessitated or involved leaving the big house, and it was only occasionally that they would venture into town. The picturesque waterfall tickled something at the back of her brain, as did the gilded clock tower that sat at the center of Main Street. The white painted gazebo looked like something out of a brochure for small town America, and she was almost positive she had sat on her father's shoulders, listening to music in the open field before the little grandstand, but those memories were hazy and indistinct.

Harper turned away from the gazebo as she passed it, not wanting to remember the way his eyes crinkled when he smiled, the conspiratorial way he would pass her a potted chocolate when she'd had a bad day, or the incense and wood smoke smell of him as he came in from the fires. Instead, she turned up the first street that intersected Main, as if she might be able to abandon her grief, leaving it at the gazebo for someone else to find.

She shuffled in and out of the tiny shops that crowded along the road, realizing that whatever it had been when she was a small child, Cambric Creek was now a thriving metropolis of boutiques and restaurants. A stone fronted shop with cathedral-like stained glass windows caught her attention, and the creaking sign above the door turned her feet inward, eyebrows raised.

To her surprise, *Viol, Violet, and Vine* turned out to be a plant shop, hardly what she had expected. She'd never excelled at herbcraft or potion making, and her thumb was as black as her wardrobe. Still, she meandered up one of the aisles, breathing in the cool, green herbaceous smell of the shop.

"Is there something I can help you find today?" The speaker was a beetle-like woman with glossy, black hair and crimson-painted lips. Two sets of arms and a pronounced cinch at the waist of the black sheath dress she wore, but her legs, from what Harper could see, appeared mostly human-like. "Anything specific you're hunting for?"

Peace and quiet. The ability to turn off my brain without having to think or feel anything. A shiny new life with two alive parents and a hundred percent less clinical depression, if you have it in stock? Instead of saying any of the things she was thinking, Harper forced her lips into a wan smile. "Just looking. I-I didn't know what kind of shop this was when I came in."

"Just looking is the best way to find exactly what you're looking for," the shop attendant tittered, smiling broadly.

"With plants especially. The fastest way to go home with a full cart is to come in only intending to take a look around."

"I've actually got a bit of a black thumb," Harper confessed with an uncomfortable laugh. "I used to help my mother in the greenhouse when I was young . . ." She swallowed hard, remembering the small jam jars of spider plants and pothos cuttings she was responsible for, having serious conversations with tender new shoots, spritzing them with a small mister. Her sister had been a colicky infant, and she recognized now that it had likely been a good way for her mother to keep Harper occupied and not underfoot, as she dealt with a cranky baby. "That-that was a long time ago, though. I'm afraid I wouldn't be a very good plant parent to any of these."

"Oh, I'm not so sure about that. I'll bet there's a succulent here with your name on it."

Harper was unable to hold back an outraged bark of laughter. "Succulents are the worst! Everyone claims you can't kill them, but I have proven that wisdom wrong many, many times." She gestured to the shelves of small stone dishes containing the green marauders. "These would be the first to go, I'm telling you."

The beetle woman laughed, a delicate, tinkling sound that carried across the room, thanks to the cavernous cathedral ceiling. A door swung open on the opposite wall, and an identical beetle woman clicked out, placing what sounded like an order for shipping boxes on the Bluetooth hooked over her ear before disappearing again up another aisle. Sisters, obviously. *Twins*.

"Succulents are introverts," the sister before her continued. "That's the mistake so many folks make. They hear 'succulents are easy' and feel as if they have something to prove, because they don't want to be the one who killed the unkillable plant. And then they overcompensate. Succulents want to be left alone to enjoy the sunshine and meditate on their existence, but too many would-be plant stewards over socialize them. Over watered, over moved, over fussed with. All they want is alone time. Not that difficult at all, as long as you respect their need for solitude."

She had never felt kinship with any thing or any being as much as she did with the eye-level little dish of spiky, jade-green rosettes, but Harper knew herself too well. She was too numb, too neglectful, too unqualified for even the most basic responsibility. She would fail the little plant, and it would die. It would be one more failure to add to her collection, one more disappointment, and she would be crushed under the weight of them. Ilea's voice, catty and smug, still rattled in her ears. *Failing at things is second nature at this point*. She didn't need to waste her money on one more thing she'd spoil with her ineptitude. *Fucking Ilea*.

"I can't be trusted, believe me. You don't want any of your plants going home with me."

The beetle woman fixed her with an appraising gaze before shrugging with a small smile.

"What was it that brought you through our doors, then? Not that you can't look around," she hastily added, "please, take your time. I'm just being nosy."

The woman turned away to let Harper kill time in peace. She should have made her way back up the aisle and out the door, but the words were itching to come out and complete the line.

"Resignedly beneath the sky, the melancholy waters lie."

The beetle woman turned back, eyebrow arched, with a crimson smile. "You're no caretaker of plants, but you *are* a lover of literature."

Harper shrugged, reddening. "I-I just want to find some-place quiet to read my book. The library was closed and the coffee shop was packed. I saw your sign and thought maybe you were a bookshop . . . I wouldn't have guessed a plant store, but I probably should have."

"Arboratory," the still smiling woman corrected. "We're far more than a store that sells plants. You should try Azathé, they're just another door down. It's. . . sort of a tea shop."

"Sort of?"

The beetle woman laughed, shrugging gracefully. Her slender neck and collarbone were an iridescent green, and the set of arms not engaged in the conversation straightened the little stone dishes on the shelf. "It's part curiosity shop, part divination, and they serve tea. It's a bit odd, but rather quaint." Her eyes gave Harper a fast, up-and-down appraisal. "I think you'll actually like it quite a bit, it matches your aesthetic. And the coffee shop is *always* that crowded."

"I prefer tea anyway," she murmured, beginning to drift slowly to the door. "Thank you for the information, I appreciate it."

"Of course! And remember — if you're ever looking to add a fellow introvert to your life, we have a wide selection."

✦ · · ✦ · ✦ · · ✦ · · ✦ · · · ✦ · · ✦

The sound of the bell above the tea shop's door could not be classified as a tinkle. For that matter, Harper wasn't sure it could even be called a bell.

A twisted hunk of metal hung above the doorway in the place of where a tinkling bell would be in a different establishment, and the sound it made—a toneless clang into the void—seemed to cause the air in the small shop to palpably shiver and shake. Harper squinted as she looked up at it, able to make out the etching of what she assumed was the name of the manufacturer. *Enchantment. Joke's on them. This is a terrible bell.*

Her eyes continued past the twisted hunk of junk to the wall behind it — too high for anyone but an orc or ogre to see at eye level, a ridiculous place to hang anything, let alone a photograph, but a photograph was what was there. A black and white photograph of a ship, a long steamer, and beside it, her collected crew. *The SS Yeoman's Enchantment.* Her eyebrows drew together. *What the actual fuck?* This wasn't a bell at all, she realized, but a part of the ship in the photograph.

Harper wondered what the significance was, but before she could pull out her phone to investigate, a tufty-eared cat appeared from the small hostess stand, determinedly rubbing its head against her shins. Black with silvery-white points, the cat wound around her black boots, vocalizing insistently until she was in danger of tripping.

"Hello! Calm down, okay? Hi there, pretty girl." The cat preened as she stroked her palm down its sleek back, spine arching and legs stretching before it seemed to remember itself. Meowing again, it trotted forward a few paces, looking back at her expectantly.

The host stand was comprised of a small podium that held an automatic checkout kiosk, but no actual host in sight. Harper spotted the thick, tufted cushion where the cat had sprung from, shaking her head silently. *That's a great way to have your cat go darting out the door into traffic. What are they thinking?!* She wished, not for the first time, that Ilea possessed an average cat's desire to go scooting out of doors to explore the outside world. *I'd never let them back in.*

No employee had emerged, and she frowned, unsure of what she ought to do. The cat abruptly changed course, circling back to move behind her, headbutting at the back of her ankles, continuing to mewl.

"Hey! What are you, a sheepdog? Should you even be in here?"

When it darted past her a second time, glancing over its shoulder and yowling authoritatively, she shrugged, deciding it must have been a 'seat yourself' establishment. *There are bossy cats bullying you everywhere you go, apparently*. Her mouth opened to address the cat as she stepped away from the host stand to cross over the dining room's threshold, but her words dried up, leaving her gaping.

Tall, cathedral-like windows lined the far wall, and she could see at the very back of the space a glassed-in ceiling, like an old-fashioned conservatory. The dining room was barely lit, and the sun was already too high in the sky for the Eastern-facing windows to allow sunlight to pour into the space. It gave the dining room a dim, heavily shadowed aura, one that complemented the decor in the most macabre way she could have ever imagined.

Towers of precariously stacked books dotted the space in between small tables that were hardly large enough for two people to squeeze around. Everywhere she turned, books were stacked in twisting staircase-like spires — on the floor, on shelves, on the edges of mantles. In between the books were curiosities that would not have been out of place on the recipe shelf of a high crone's potion station. Pinned moths and butterflies, taxidermized owls and tarantulas and bats, set in odd little tableaux — chicks wearing pinafore dresses, sitting at miniature tea tables with a giant spider, and just above, what appeared to be a wolpertinger sitting beside a dagger on a raised plinth, its blade wearing a film of what looked to be dried blood.

Harper stepped into the room slowly, realizing at once there were other patrons in attendance. A young woman with thick glasses and a tumble of long, seaweed-like green hair sat at a tiny table with her nose buried in a book, and on the opposite end of the dining room, a pair of nymphs were in quiet conversation. Neither paid her any mind.

She paused at the first table she passed, startled to realize it was a spirit board. Intricately painted, with a black lacquered planchette at its center. The next table was a black pedestal and waxed blonde wood, bearing the outlined template for a three-card tarot spread. She grinned, understanding why the beetle woman next door said this place would fit Harper's aesthetic. *This is a goth wonderland.*

Needle-point chairs and chintz poufs were nestled in amongst grimoires and artful piles of animal skulls, half-burned candles, and voodoo dolls, a mason jar full of needles, and against the opposite wall, a dessert case featuring colorful macarons and glacéed fruit tarts, delicious and completely out of place. *Or completely in place, because why does it have to be one thing or the other?* There were cut flowers, both fresh and dried, and increasingly long shadows as she moved further into the room. The interior was a curious mix of English garden and a mad witch's fever dream, and she had never before felt as enamored with a place purely based on the optics, but Harper found herself wondering if she might be able to rent space in one of the corners and never go home.

The little cat yowled again, rather insistently, drawing her attention to a small table in the corner. The bossy feline seemed impatient with her as she slowly pulled out a chair, deciding the cat had chosen well enough for her.

"Okay, okay. I'm going to sit here, all right? You know, this place seems cool, but the service is awfully pushy." Her words were in jest, but as of yet, she had still not seen a single employee of the establishment other than this presumptuous little cat. She draped her bag over the back of the chair after removing her book, and the beast seemed mollified. Before Harper was able to deliver one final scratch behind the ears, it trotted back to its cushion at the host stand, curling up contentedly.

The table the cat had led her to possessed a quill and a small pot of ink, the tabletop itself covered in a scroll of parchment paper. *How curious.* A shelf just above eye level held a line of numbered books, and an inspection of their spines showed it was a series entitled *Deadly Beauty: The Care and Keeping of Poisonous Flowers*. Beside the books rested a small bowl of incense, a glowing red candle, and what appeared to be a monkey's paw.

At the edge of the table was a small journal, and upon inspection, she realized it was the tea menu. She paged through the book slowly — spice-filled black teas, Ceylon gold, twenty-year-aged pu'erh, delicate floral-dotted whites, fruit-filled greens, classic breakfast blends alongside silver needle jasmine pearls, more teas than she could count. She would need to live one hundred years to sample every item on this menu, she considered.

The vast tea selection was a sign the proprietors obviously knew their business well, but she had always been someone who was overwhelmed by choices, and as she paged through the menu, the different teas began to blur together, indistinct and inseparable until she was unable to recount a single flavor profile the instant her eyes left the description, the words on the page a meaningless slurry. There was still no sign of any employee who might make a recommendation, and so Harper found herself seeking out something safe and familiar. A green wellness blend she'd had before, many times before. That would do.

She made a point of closing the menu and replacing it on the edge of the table, making it exceedingly obvious, she thought, that she'd made her choice and was ready to place her order. Still, no server appeared. As the minutes ticked by, she began to fidget in her seat, glancing around the dining room, waiting for a server to come bumbling out of the back room, perhaps covered in flour from a dessert mishap or dripping in water from a burst pipe, *something* that would explain away their long absence from the front end of the restaurant, but no one was forthcoming.

Sighing heavily, she opened her book. *You planned on going to the library. It's not like afternoon tea was ever the plan. Just read your book in peace and quiet until they kick you out.* She *was* a bit peckish, though. There was usually an energy bar or two floating around her bag, Harper reminded herself, and that would suffice if necessary. *Maybe you order from that little kiosk at the front. Maybe this is a self-service place?*

She was just about to push her chair back to investigate when the cat abruptly bounced onto the tabletop, yowling in her face. Harper jumped, gasping. The tiny beast hissed, swiping at the quill, giving her a disgusted look before leaping from the table, stalking off imperiously with its tail in the air. She didn't know what kind of place this was, but she was *done* with cats treating her so poorly.

*It acted as though you're meant to do something with the quill. As if it **knew** you were meant to do something with the quill . . .* Her mind felt sluggish, as if it had spent too long wrapped in a quagmire of blankets and sorrow, and it struggled to kick itself free, synapses misfiring before sparking to life at last. She sucked in a sharp breath. *Holy shit. Does the fucking cat **work** here? Is **that** the employee?*

She gave the dining room another swift appraisal. The two nymphs were still deep in conversation, the green-haired girl now highlighting sections of her book. There was no server, no host, no one. Shadows, the odd bric-a-brac filling the place, and the little cat, and no one else. *What the fuck kind of place is this?!* She envisioned a kitchen full of apron-clad felines, brewing tea and rolling out pastries ineffectually with their small paws, bickering over tiny cakes.

She took up the quill, feeling a bit foolish, hesitating for a long moment before dipping it into the ink.

I'd like the green wellness tea.

She hesitated again, wondering if the place even had a regular menu.

I don't know if you have food, but I wouldn't say no to a chicken salad sandwich.

Please, she added hastily.

As she watched, the ink sunk into the rich parchment, spreading slightly before disappearing completely. Harper sat back in her chair, biting her lip. *What the actual fuck.* She had no idea what kind of establishment this was and didn't know why she was taking orders from fucking cats. *Oh well. If you get your tea, great. If not, at least it's somewhere quiet to read your book. That's all you wanted in the first place.*

Harper didn't know whether this would be classified as one more thing at which she had failed, but one thing was certain — she was already exhausted, and it was barely mid-day. She didn't have to put her brain to work when she was cocooned in her bed, and it had been weeks since she'd had to do this much thinking. *No, this isn't your fault. What kind of place is run by a cat?!*

Losing herself in the pages of her book, she almost didn't notice the small tea cart rolling out of a previously unnoticed back room a short while later, pushed by invisible hands.

Harper startled when it stopped beside her table, realizing the cart held a steaming pot of tea, a dainty teacup and saucer, a silver strainer and bowl, and a small plate of phyllo cups, each filled with a scoop of chicken salad. She wondered if the cart was on some sort of automatic timer, realizing if that were the case, it might abruptly reverse course and disappear back to the kitchen, taking her lunch along with it. Carefully maneuvering to avoid any embarrassing spills, she moved the items from the tea cart to her small table, and sure enough, a moment later, the cart rolled away. *Okay, this place is fucking bananas. But so, so cool.*

There was something about the shadow in this place — long and cool and dark, stretching from wall to wall — that put her at ease. It was just mid-afternoon, and the outside world would be bright and bustling, demanding too much. To be cheerful and sociable when all she wanted to do was hide away until the empty pit in her chest had filled itself in, instead of echoing with every breath she took, a reminder that she was not good enough. The dimly lit, shadowed interior of this bizarre little tea house was like a cozy cave, one filled with oddities like her. Harper wondered if the cat would even notice if she placed herself on one of the shelves, taking her spot amongst the headless dolls and taxidermied bats and other ephemera too imperfect for the outside world.

More than two hours had passed by the time she closed her book with a snap, realizing she still needed to catch the bus back home, which might mean navigating her way around downtown. *Back home to the daily lecture*. The tea cart had reappeared after the first hour, bearing a fresh pot of hot water for her tea and a small cream puff on a doily-covered saucer. *A cat restaurant with excellent service. Who could have guessed?*

There was a small number at the corner of the table, and sure enough, once she had packed up her bag and made her way to the checkout kiosk at the hostess stand, she was able to tap in her table number and bring up her bill. Harper felt vaguely ridiculous leaving a generous tip for a cat, but it had been the most enjoyable afternoon she'd spent in Cambric Creek since her move, and she couldn't wait to return to the strange little tea house with the bossy feline hostess and invisible staff. Yelled at by a cat, again, but at least it wasn't her mother's cat. *Fucking Ilea.*

It was, she realized as she trudged up the sidewalk, wincing in the blistering sunlight, the first time she had gone out on her own since sobbing over the creamsicles. She had made a promise to her sister that she was going to try. She didn't know how to break it to Morgan that she was a lost cause, had proven that time and time again in the past year and a half, but if nothing else, she was a failure of her word. *You promised Morgan you were going to try. That you would get out of the house. Well, now you have someplace to go.*

The thought of returning to the house that was not home didn't fill her with joy, and now that she was awake, Harper realized the rest of the day and evening stretched before her, and she would need to find something to do to fill the hours. *See, this is why it's just easier to get up at three p.m.* She didn't know what she was going to do with herself, but she had made a promise to her sister, and she intended to keep it. She didn't know what tomorrow held other than the fact that she would most definitely be coming back to this strange little tea shop and the bossy little cat.

Chapter 4

OTD: Fishnets. Short-sleeved sailor dress. Death Head moth barrettes. Lunar cycle backpack. When life gives you heartache, give it back a jaunty collar.

The second time she visited the little tearoom, she was better prepared. The little cat bounced from her cushion as Harper came through the door, the heavy clang of the twisted hunk of metal announcing her arrival.

The *SS Yeoman's Enchantment* had gone down on a large, icy lake more than twenty years before she'd even been born. A freak storm, the website she'd consulted reported — one minute, the large steamer showed on the radar, and the next, it was gone, lost to the frozen depths. The ship and her crew had never been recovered. *And yet.* The bell above the door bore the clear markings of the ship's name. She desperately wanted to ask how the shop's proprietor had acquired such a maritime souvenir. *Scuba diving cats, maybe?*

Following the cat through the small entryway into the dining room, she noticed again there were only one or two other patrons. Her table, the one with the scroll, was empty once more.

"D-do you mind?" She murmured to the little cat, feeling vaguely ridiculous as she gestured to the table. "I-I suppose I'm a creature of habit."

The cat mewled, hesitating with a glance to a spirit board table, the one it had been leading her to, evidently deciding her request was one it was willing to accommodate. It gave her a bossy yowl as she pulled back her chair as if reminding her of the way things worked last time, an indication she should not sit there waiting endlessly.

"I know, I know. Write my order on the scroll. I remember."

She told herself that morning as she left her cottage that she was going to take time every day to explore Cambric Creek, either before or after her teahouse sojourn. *No time for lunch today. Have your tea, read your book, and then keep walking the other way down the block to see what's there. Maybe you'll find another little café. Maybe there's a shop around here like the one with the auction. You could get a job there and actually have a reason to get up every morning. Who knows, maybe you'll be good at it. They'll actually appreciate your attention to detail when it comes to matching shades of black and will make you a manager.* It would make sense if such a shop existed, for all of the curiosities aligning the shelves and cluttering up the space in the team room had to have come from somewhere.

The green wellness tea, please. Her order was ironic, she thought darkly. It wasn't as if the tea was magically going to make her well again, no matter how much she guzzled.

Her only plan was to get out of the house. Make herself scarce at home, preventing her mother from pulling her into service as her lackey as she fussed with her crystals. Crystals and stones were her mother's chosen tools of the craft and for as long as she could remember, every full moon and new moon would see her mother outside in the middle of the night, laying out crystals charged, dropping them in vases of rainwater, wrapping them in herbs. Crystals wrapped in warm, wet towels, placed on her forehead when she was sick, nestled beneath her pillow to chase away bad dreams, worry stones slipped into her book bag as an overly anxious child.

Harper never had an affinity for the bits of colorful rock, much to her mother's disappointment. Morgan had stepped up in her place, learning the uses for every crystal, how to charge them, how to apply them, how to use them to banish or attract. Her mother was currently going through all of her crystals and stones, checking for damage or discoloration, replacing those deemed unworthy, re-cataloguing each and every one in her collection, which was vast. Harper had no desire to be a part of the chore.

Her plan for the day had worked, as little of a plan as it was. By the time she got home that afternoon — after she had lost herself in her book once more, realizing that her commitment to go exploring would have to wait another day — the driveway was empty, and she was able to scurry up the gravel unseen, slipping into her little cottage like a mouse. The rest of the afternoon and evening stretched before her, but she had gone out. Her version of trying was not what her mother would have approved, no doubt, and possibly not what Morgan had in mind when she made her request, but that, too, didn't matter, Harper decided. Trying was bound to look different for everyone.

+ · · · + · · · + · · · + · + · · + · + · · +

OOTD: Lace skirt. Puffed sleeve blouse. Existential panic. Grommeted boots with oxblood laces.

By the fourth time she stepped through the doorway at Azathé, Harper felt like a regular. The little cat attempted to shepherd her to different tables each time, giving up when Harper still moved to the table with the scroll. She didn't like not knowing what to do, and in the absence of a direct order, she would fall back on what was familiar and comfortable.

The first afternoon she entered and found the dining room empty, she took advantage of the momentary solitude to explore the space a bit closer. Totems and statuettes of different deities from cultures all around the world lined the shelves, in between the taxidermied animals and skulls. Books on witchcraft, on sorcery, on every facet of the occult lay nestled in between tomes of Shakespeare, poetry books from the 1800s, classics bound in cloth and leather, fiction and nonfiction resting side-by-side with little organization. At least, not that she could make sense of.

A jar of four-leaf clovers sat beside a stack of different tarot decks, Lapis blue eyes peering out from a dozen different points throughout the room, all there to ward away the evil eye. On one shelf rested a small gem-encrusted jewelry box filled with the type of poison rings her sister had admired on the auction's website. Ceremonial candles and altar tools, a small shelf of irradiated sugar bowls, teacups of different sizes and shapes and patterns in between all the ephemera. *I wonder where they get their stuff.* By the time the cart arrived with her tea, she had walked around the entire room, giving each corner a cursory exploration.

You should sit down and look at the course booklet. While waiting for her trolley earlier in the week, she'd passed a display for the local college outside the community center. *Dozens of graduate programs on offer! Become a Master of planning your future today!* A large QR code for the school's enrollment website and a box of booklets listing the different courses offered sat just beneath the pronouncement, and she'd pulled one from the box, still riding a brief wave of optimism from that afternoon's teahouse sojourn.

By the time she was back on her own sofa, paging through the booklet, she was overwhelmed by the choices. Her mother had never been the one she'd gone to for help parsing through options, least of all for something important and likely very expensive like this. *She's more likely to tell you it's not worth the money for you to flunk out of something else.*

She should sit and page through the booklet again . . . but it was self-care to take a time-out when needed, right? And she had been told to focus on self-care. . . *No sense in letting your tea go cold*, she told herself, pulling out her book and turning off her mind.

✦ · · · ✦ · · ✦ · · ✦ · · · ✦ · · ✦ · · · ✦

OOTD: Black dress. Black knee socks. Black bat earrings and matching bow. Ouija tote bag for all your negative confirmation bias. Patent ankle boots.

She had yet to explore the town. Every time she sat at the familiar scroll table and pulled out her book, buffeted in the long, thick shadows that stretched across the length of the dining room, time stopped, that insidious little voice in her head tamped back, and Harper couldn't bring herself to end her stupor prematurely to do something as inconsequential as get to know her new home. *Home is a word that doesn't mean anything. Home is gone. Nothing will ever feel like home again.*

The sentiment was underscored by the conversation she had happened upon earlier that week. Harper avoided the big house as much as possible, avoiding her mother being the true aim, but she'd been in the wrong place at the wrong time — standing outside the door to her cottage when a frazzled courier came screeching to the curb at the end of the long driveway. She might have become completely antisocial in the past year and a half, but she still couldn't bring herself to be rude, particularly to people just trying to do their jobs. The slender mothman had already seen her, and she couldn't very well go scurrying back indoors and ignoring him, not once he was bustling up the driveway, a box under his arm. Once the truck had lurched from the curb, she had trudged up to the house with her mother's delivery.

"I just wish I knew what to do to help her. Help her re-find her focus, help her decide what she's going to do with her life . . . help her do *some*thing."

She'd stood stock still, holding her breath. *Maybe,* she told herself, *they're not even talking about you. Maybe this entire conversation is about one of her crystals.* The hope was dashed a heartbeat later, Ilea, as usual, delivering the fatal blow.

"There's no shame in only having one of them be a witch," they purred. "Morgan will do perfectly well on her beginner qualification exams. It's like what the royals say — an heir and a spare, right? Focus your energy on where the potential is. Especially with the new coven. You want to show that the Hollingsworth witches deserve a seat in the inner circle, right? Evelyn doesn't suffer fools gladly, and I can't think of anything more foolish than wasting your precious time on someone who's shown they don't want to be helped. More than that, even — beyond help. I don't think there's any rule on who the *spare* needs to be in this equation."

She didn't bother waiting to hear how her mother might respond. Leaving the package on the countertop, Harper had slipped from the house, not pausing to wipe away the tears burning at her eyes until the cottage door slammed behind her.

You're a lost cause, beyond help. Your own mother thinks so. She wasn't sure what she was bothering to try for, not that she was doing a particularly good job in the first place. Her family had been through enough those past two years, and she wanted Morgan and her mother to be happy. She wanted them to thrive in this new, stricter coven . . . and that wouldn't happen if she was around to spoil everything, all the time, at every turn. It would be easier to slip beneath the surface of the waves in this desolate sea, letting the undertow pull her until her family was relieved of the burden of her.

+ · · · + · · · + · · · + · · · + · · · + · · · +

OOTD: Black dress. Black shoes, black bag. Black heart, black soul, like a stain that ought to be washed away.

The seventh time she visited the tearoom, she didn't bother tip-toeing around the dining room to examine the collection of oddities, didn't exclaim in delight over antique copies of her favorite books or wonder who was wishing on the monkey's paw that was steadily counting down fingers. She ignored the little cat, who mewled protestingly as she entered the dining room, beelining to her preferred seat to pull out her book. She was desperate to lose herself, to quiet the voice in her head, at least for a little while, until she decided if she was going to continue struggling to swim or sink at last.

The green wellness tea, please.

She dropped the quill distractedly, flipping her book open heedlessly, uncaring of the page. *The Care and Cleaning of Medieval Weapons* was not a topic that particularly interested her, not to the degree that she would choose an entire book on the subject, but it was a book from her father's shelf, one he'd pored over several dozen times that she could remember. One he'd held in his hands, when he'd still been there to remind her that bad times never lasted forever, and despite the fairness of her skin and her preference for the indoors, the sun would always break through the heavy clouds of melancholy that had enveloped her since she was a teen.

She was so distracted and eager to quiet her mind that she nearly missed the words that bled up from the parchment.

We have over a hundred different loose-leaf selections.

Harper blinked in confusion as the words appeared beneath her own. *Maybe it's an ad. Some automated response.* She bit her lip, taking up the quill. *The green wellness tea. Please.* To her shock, the writing continued, dispelling her assumption of an automated advertisement.

If you are interested in blade craft, there are some excellent selections on the shelf above the mounted wolpertinger.

The green wellness tea, she tried again.

I would suggest a flinty Pu'er to complement the

"I just want the green wellness tea."

Her voice seemed over-loud in the quiet dining room, flummoxed that the scroll was talking to her like an actual flesh-and-blood server. The writing had stopped, the scroll's previous, interrupted sentence left incomplete, and for a long, yawing moment, nothing happened. Nothing more appeared on the scroll after she voiced her declaration, and Harper wondered if she was going to be served at all. *One more thing you've spoiled. You can't even order in a restaurant without fucking things up. Ilea's right. Failure ought to be an expectation by now.*

"I-I said I want the–"

"No." The voice was a hiss from the long shadows around her table, seeming to rise up from the floor, curling and settling around her shoulders until she'd shivered.

"But–"

"You're not allowing yourself to enjoy the unique experience here," it continued. "I really have to intervene. Now, is your interest in blade craft purely academic? There are some interesting instructional tomes on forging right over—"

"My father was a bladesmith," she blurted, unsure of why she was responding to the shadowed corner across the table as if there was a flesh and blood server standing before her. "He made beautiful weapons. Like, by hand, at a forge. I-I took fencing in school, but I don't know anything about bladecraft. I mean, I *do*, because I grew up around it, but like . . . academically. Not in practice. He's dead now."

Heat enveloped her, and tears burned at her eyes. Harper realized she was babbling. She didn't know why she was telling the empty corner about her father. She was unsure of why she was indulging the mysterious voice from the darkness. *You shouldn't be talking to the shadows at all!* And they certainly should *not* have been talking back, let alone scolding her for being a boring, predictable order.

"I see," the voice slid and curled like a serpent as it mused. "I am terribly sorry for your loss. Was it recent?"

She was unable to talk about her father without crying. She had learned as a teen that her overly emotional responses were too big, too much, making everyone around her un-comfortable, starting with her grandmother, and so she tried to avoid them. She couldn't talk about her father without crying, and so she avoided talking about him at all costs, for there would be no emotional response as big and noisy and mortifying as the ocean of grief that rocked inside her. *Too late.* The tears were already falling.

"N-no. It was l-last year."

A sigh, like a whorl of smoke around her. "That is incredibly recent, little one. Barely a moment ago. Did you help him in his forge when he worked? When you were younger?"

"I-I did." Her throat was still thick and her cheeks were still damp, but the admission made the corners of her mouth life, in spite of herself. "I would hand him tools. I'll always love the smell of hot coals and woodsmoke, I think. I didn't know the books here were things we could read?" She sucked in a deep breath, desperately trying to redirect herself, to avert her emotions, an exercise she'd practiced with her mother a hundred million times.

"Yes, you can. Yes, I think I understand very well now. Let's see . . . how long are you planning on staying with us?"

Her jaw hung open as she floundered, unable to speak, despite her verbal deluge of thirty seconds prior, wondering if the voice was able to divine the question that had been hanging over her since she overheard the conversation between her mother and Ilea. *How long are you planning on staying with us? That's anyone's guess.*

"Do you have someplace to be?" the voice tried again. It, whatever it was, asked the question as if it were changing tactics, attempting to cajole her into actually answering like a normal person.

Whether she ought to have been talking to it or not, the strange voice had a dark resonance that pressed her into her seat and made her stomach swoop. She ought to be frightened, ought to be cautious and looking for an escape, but Harper couldn't deny she was intrigued, her black thoughts momentarily abating.

"I never have any place to be," she choked out on a scoff, listening as the strange voice harrumphed.

"Well then, that informs our selection for the day, does it not? There, just past that ivory candelabra . . . go on, it's not going to jump off the shelf on its own."

She realized belatedly the strange, curling voice was giving her a direction, and there was little she loved more than being told what to do, freed from the chore of thinking and making decisions. Jumping up, Harper hurried to obey. It was strange taking orders from a menu, but that didn't stop her from doing exactly what it said.

"Here?"

"Yes, right there. On the shelf above it. There's a red-bound book . . . yes, that's the one. Good girl. Now, settle in. Page 327. I'll get your tea started."

If she were anywhere else, she might have been mortified by the way her spine shivered, her core clenching. *You were just blubbering thirty seconds ago!* Perhaps, she considered, it was because of her emotional outburst. She felt raw and oversensitive, so it should have been no surprise that she was reacting to every bit of stimuli. Calling her a *good girl* was the fastest way to drench her panties, and doing so in combination with freeing her from the arduous task of thinking was her personal catnip.

Harper hurried to reseat herself, flipping open the book to the page they'd instructed. *Blood of Thine Father*. Her eyebrows drew together. The thick, leather-bound book was a collection of novella-length stories, all written in some early, archaic form of English, but one she was able to parse easily enough. It was a tale of vengeance and loss and ultimate victory, and as the tea cart arrived, bearing a steaming pot and a small three-tiered tray of sweets and savories, the rest of the afternoon passed in wonder.

Cucumber cream cheese rounds and salmon puffs, a lavender-iced cream scone, and a steaming hot pot. She wondered again if the cat would notice if she simply tucked into the shadows and declined to leave at closing.

She was happy to let someone else be in charge for a change. She enjoyed the book and, surprisingly, enjoyed the smoky tea. It didn't have a flavor she particularly liked and it certainly wasn't something she would have chosen for herself, but that hadn't mattered as she'd read, tasting the flintiness of steel kissing steel, the coldness of the dungeon keep and the rain pelting her face as she finally made it to freedom at the story's end, father avenged and family honor restored. The flavor of the aged tea had enhanced the setting, the savories were nibbled anxiously, and her scone enjoyed during the story's tender moments. It was the sort of book her father would have enjoyed, and she was glad she was there in the strange little tearoom to enjoy it in his stead, instead of bobbing along in the glass-like sea of despair.

It was strange, she thought — talking about him with the menu had poked the narrowest pinprick into the thick callus of her grief, a sliver of light over the horizon of her ocean. As she packed her bag that day, she did so with a smile tugging her lips, the first time she could remember smiling without forcing her mouth into the action in she couldn't remember how long.

"I hope you'll be back soon," the voice whispered as she gathered her things that day, bringing heat to her cheeks at its nearness.

"I will," she quickly agreed. "And-and thank you for the recommendation. It was perfect."

Harper turned out of the tea shop, and instead of heading back in the direction of the trolley stop, she turned the other way up the street, looping around the block. There was a lingerie boutique and a small 'coming soon' placard in a window bearing a leaping black rabbit. A jeweler, a small clothing boutique, and a bevy of restaurants, including a dim sum quick service counter that provided the dumplings she purchased for dinner.

You used to make your own, and they were so good. You should pull out the steamer baskets and find a recipe. Maybe this week.

It was the first time she could remember in weeks that she did not head home with lead feet. She was pleased with her tentative explorations as she boarded the trolley that would take her back to Oldetowne and vowed to turn up the other block the following afternoon. *Who knows? Maybe you can get a job in one of these little shops.*

As she came home from her nightly walk through the twilight-lit streets of the neighborhood that evening, the sight of her mother's house didn't fill her with dread as she walked

up the gravel, kicking aside some rocks that had been dis-
turbed at her front door. As she did so, Harper felt something
dislodge from around her foot, as if a part of her boot had
been kicked away. There was nothing there, but she nearly
rolled her ankle on one of the stones, annoyingly scattered
across the pathway as if something had been digging beside
her front door. *Probably chipmunks.*

It had been, she thought with another small smile, dropping exhaustedly onto her loveseat, a surprisingly good day,
the first she could remember having since her world had
upended. *Tomorrow, maybe you'll stop for a coffee first; people
watch a bit. These are your neighbors, after all. And then you let
the little cat sit you wherever it wants. Clearly, they know better.*

Normally, admitting she knew less than a small, bossy
cat would be humiliating, another mark of imperfection and
failure . . . but in this case, it only made her smile broadly,
wondering what tea she'd be served tomorrow.

Chapter 5

*O*OTD: Ribbed cotton midi-length slip dress and flip flops.
Evil eye talisman hairpin. Satin Raven lipstain. Owl
head handbag. Fun, fresh, fabulous.

There was a man knocking at her door.

Harper flattened herself to the wall at the first rap of
his knuckles to the wood, her heart thumping, relieved
she'd been in the small kitchen at the time instead of her
normal place curled on the sofa. In general, the presence
of a stranger knocking at her door would not have been
enough to induce her panic — it wasn't as if she didn't
do most of her shopping online, after all. But this man
was knocking at her back door, the back door to her little
cottage, when the main house was looming just ahead.

*That meant he had to walk past the house and around the side
of the cottage. He's probably trying to break in.* She'd listened
to enough true crime podcasts to know that being home
during a daytime home invasion was a one-way ticket to her
remains being found in an abandoned field, identifiable only

through dental records. *And that orthodontist was a quack, so who even knows what your dental records say.*

She might laugh at herself later, but at that moment, gripping a steak knife and sliding down the wall seemed the most prudent course of action. *Get on the ground. People only pay attention to things at eye level. Put yourself beneath that, and he won't even notice you until you're slicing his ankle open with the steak knife.*

Peeking around the short partition from where she knelt on the kitchen floor, she hoped the man had given up, but he was still there — a black-clad figure, only slightly visible through the sidelight windows . . . windows he, she realized in horror, was bending to peer through. Black hair and a close-cropped beard, his nose practically pressed to the wavy, century-old glass as he looked into her home, his gaze immediately casting down. He exclaimed triumphantly, and she squeaked, their eyes meeting through the window from where she peered up from the floor, caught out, despite her best effort. *See, this is the problem. Even your best effort is trash.*

For several long moments, Harper remained as still as a statue, wondering if she could pass herself off a creepy doll left abandoned on the floor. Her hopes were dashed as the man knocked insistently, staring at her through the window.

She groaned, admitting defeat as she pushed herself back to an upright position, tightening her grip on the knife.

"The state of the world is in sorry shape," the man began the instant the door cracked open, "if lurking on the floor is preferable to greeting a neighbor."

Harper stiffened at his brazen audacity. *You open the door for an uninvited stranger, and there's a lecture waiting on the other side. Fucking typical.*

"You know," he went on peevishly, "a generation ago, people used to actually come to the door when there was someone knocking."

"Yeah, and serial killers were prevalent at the exact same time. I wonder why. Were you banging on my back door for a reason? Or just to be a bit of a dick?" He scowled, and she glowered, his lip peeling back slightly to reveal over-long canines, as her hand tightened around the handle of her knife.

"This is the front door, girl. See? Sidelights, decorative mullions. Look at the scroll work on those hinges." He sniffed imperiously, and Harper wondered if she had just cause at that point to slash him with the steak knife. Twisting out the door, she examined the decorative hinges he called out, frowning when she realized he was right.

"Hey!" She yelped as the man pulled the door open and elbowed past her, letting himself into her home as confidently as if he were the one who lived there. *A strange man just forced his way into your house, stab him! There's no jury that would convict you!* The man glanced back as if he could hear her thoughts, eyes flashing, thoroughly unconcerned. *Unconcerned because he's probably about to pull out a recipe to cook your liver.*

To add insult to injury, he had the nerve to be handsome. He was average height, with pale skin and sharp cheekbones, thick raven-colored hair, his eyes lined in jet, head-to-toe immaculate goth aesthetic, right down to the silver serpent latchets on his black boots. *Great, so he's an attractive serial killer. I'm pretty sure they all work the same way.*

The only thing about him that gave her significant pause — aside from the fact that he'd just forced his way into her home, completely uninvited — were his eyes. Citrine green, striking, and completely inhuman. Cat-like. Harper gulped. She'd seen eyes like his before, saw them every time she was forced into her mother's home. *Fucking Ilea.*

"Anyway," he breezed, as casually as if they'd been making small talk about the weather. "I'm looking for Mau. They're a contemporary of mine."

"Yeah, I don't know who that is." Harper shrugged, attempting to block him from making it any further into the cottage. "Guess you ought to be going." He ducked around her easily.

"I always loved this house," the man hummed, turning slowly, completely ignoring her. "It's been years since I've been inside."

"Wait, you've been here before? Were you invited, or were you trespassing then, too?"

He grinned, his long canines gleaming. "Oh, I was a guest. The witch who lived here would host the most excellent gatherings for sisters of the coven. Deipnon, solstice, casting sessions . . . the food was always excellent, and we would dance until the sky lightened. Pernella knew how to throw a party. There was never a question of that. Mau? Ilemauzer? As I said, they're a contemporary. They're of the . . . feline persuasion, if you will."

"Ilea. Their name is Ilea."

The man snorted, rolling his eyes. "Is that what they're calling themselves these days? No matter. Where can I find them?"

Harper grit her teeth. She wasn't Ilea's personal assistant, and she didn't care for this attractive, gothic man's assumption that she would jump to aid him. "They live in the main house. Not here. So, like I said, you should go. Wait, you knew my Great Aunt Pernella? How?"

Her grandmother's sister had been *an eccentric*, as she'd been told as a child. A solitary witch who practiced alone,

isolated from the coven, and most unwelcome at gatherings. At least, according to her grandmother.

The man was too young to have known her great-aunt.
Let alone to have partied with her. She swallowed down
a snort at the thought. He looked to be no older than
his early thirties at most, but if he was like Ilea . .
. Harper gulped again. Familiars were tricky creatures.
Shapeshifters possessing no true power of their own, acting as conduits for witches to realize and enhance their
abilities . . . but this man *did* possess power, she could tell,
and the longer she looked at him, the greater and more
obvious it seemed. The vibration of magic within him was
so strong that he nearly wavered at his edges. Perhaps
it was merely the effect of the form he assumed, but he
seemed like a witch in his own right, at least to her. *He
definitely doesn't look like he'd be following anyone around
with a headset and a clipboard.*

"I did indeed. My witch was often a guest of hers."

"You're a familiar then? A friend of Ilea's?"

His smile stretched, canines gleaming. "Why does, I wonder, the notion of that make you grip your little butter
knife so hard, girl?"

Heat suffused her, creeping up her neck, but she held firm.
She wouldn't have Ilea tainting her home with their poisonous tongue, and if this man was Ilea's friend, he needed to

leave. "If you're a friend of Ilea, you're not a friend of mine. So, like, it's time to get out. No offense."

He continued to grin. "None taken. The enemy of mine enemy is mine friend, is that it? Well, I suppose that makes us the best of friends. Ilemauzer is no friend of mine. Your great aunt, was it?"

Harper knew it was likely ridiculous, a consequence of her troubled mind, but his declaration made her shoulders sag in relief. If he was an enemy of Ilea's, even a superficial bitch-eating-crackers enemy, he could stay as long as he liked.

"My great-aunt, yes. My grandmother's sister. Did you know her too? My grandmother said Aunt Pernella was a bit of a shut-in? Isolated from the coven. And you didn't answer me."

The man grinned again, stepping slowly around the room, examining her things. "Yes," he answered at last, his gaze swinging from the stack of ice cream bowls collecting on her end table to her face, "I'm a familiar. I am Holt."

Something deep inside her shivered, her primal witchy center, although she didn't know why.

"I have always been Holt, and I always will be, so you never need to worry about someone barging through your door in ten years asking for me by some silly nickname. If you call for me, it will only ever be by my name."

Harper bit her lip to keep from grinning, her grip on the knife slackening. She tried to imagine herself still here in a decade, perhaps working at the tea shop, hosting the witchy parties her great aunt allegedly had, this cocksure familiar in attendance.

"And no offense to your bloodline, witchling, but your grandmother was always a little idiot. A commonplace talent, more concerned with appearances and her gossiping friends to ever be of true value to the coven. A shut-in? Pernella? Solitary? Hardly. The only group she was isolated from were the other run-of-the-mill witches with pedestrian skills."

Harper nearly choked on her outraged laughter. *Her* grandmother? Her fussy, don't sit on the good furniture, don't run—don't yell—don't breathe too strangely grand-mother? The one as preoccupied with perfection as Harper's mother? *Where do you think mom learned it?*

"Once Authricia stepped down," the cat-man went on, "your grandmother's nasty-minded little coterie of dull plod-ders took control, which is how we find ourselves in such a sorry state today. Fortunately, their time is waning." Harper gaped as he shrugged, turning away once more. "Sorry if you're extremely devoted to this coven, witchling. Like I said, no offense."

"None taken," she echoed his words with another stran-gled laugh. Since she wasn't currently enrolled in study, the coven expected her to continue attending the junior meetings, alongside teenagers, and she would sooner become a Buddhist. The notion of her haughty, hoity-toity grandmother being called a *commonplace talent* by this goth familiar positively tickled her. "Did you know my mother?"

He turned again, thick black brows coming together for a moment. "Hmmm . . . no, I don't believe I did. We were in a state of flux for a bit, my witch and I."

"She hasn't been an active member of this coven for a long time. She met my father in school, and they got married as soon as she was finished with the Collegium. They moved back to my dad's hometown, and he ran the family forge with his brother. We only moved back here recently, since . . . since he died." There it was again, that niggling little itch to give voice to the maelstrom of emotion within her. She kicked it back, hoping he didn't notice the way her voice wavered.

"And Ilemauzer belongs to her?"

"Yes. Ilea has been with her since she was a girl."

Holt sniffed. "Then I suppose she must be a slightly less pedestrian witch than your grandmother. That bodes very well for you, if we're counting backwards."

"I-I'm not so sure about that."

"Aren't you, though? You come from a long line of witch-es, some of them great ones. Are *you* not a witch, girl? Or are you only playing make-believe by dressing like one?"

Her grip tightened around the knife. Never mind that he was right. Never mind that she was barely a witch at this point, was likely as pedestrian and commonplace as her grandmother, never mind that she was a drop-out and a failure with no real future and no idea what to do with herself. She wasn't going to stand here and let some mangy, probably flea-bitten tomcat insult her *wardrobe* in her own home.

"Well, talk about pedestrian and commonplace. Is that what you think? You have eyeliner and a leather jacket, so you're some hot shit familiar? That's pretty fuckin' cringe. *This*," she gestured to herself, "is an aesthetic. It doesn't make me anything other than well-dressed. Seems like you're the only one playing dress up, cat boy. Poorly, if we're *counting backward*. I don't know what *you're* trying to do, but your shirt and your pants are two completely different colors, and neither of them is the same as your boots. Amateur effort, three out of ten. Mid. At best."

He was laughing before she had even finished. "Aesthet-ic does not make a witch. On that, we completely agree."

Harper crossed her arms, unmollified.

"And my shirt is *meant* to be lighter, I'll have you know. But that doesn't answer my question. Are you a witch or not?"

She swallowed hard, shrugging miserably, annoyed at the humiliation that filled her. *He's a familiar, an imp. He's used to dealing with real witches, not drop-outs. As soon as you tell him the truth, he's probably going to scratch your curtains and throw up in your shoe.*

"I-I don't know that I am." She laughed weakly, a pathetic, limping sound even to her own ears. "I've been in the junior coven all my life. I attended the Collegium for all of my pre-recs and cores—"

"I went to the Collegium," he interrupted her again, a wistful expression taking up residence on his handsome, angular face. "With my witch, of course. Such an excellent experience for a witchling new on her path. That's where you truly learn the meaning of sisterhood for the first time and the strength of the circle. Together, we are strong. When those bonds of sisterhood are broken, well . . . one is no different than any other human. Just with better books. What is it that you're studying?"

Harper opened her mouth to correct him, that she studied at the Collegium no longer, that she hadn't chosen a discipline, that she was the one no different from any other human, but he had whipped away, staring at an empty corner beside her loveseat. His attention was a herky-jerky thing, picking up conversation threads and abandoning them just as quickly. *Typical cat.*

He was snooping through her entire house, she realized in exasperation. Opening cupboards, peeking at the pile of mail on the table, opening her refrigerator and peering inside. *Maybe he's looking for evidence that you're even a witch. Fat chance of him finding it. Or maybe he's still deciding whether or not to kill you.*

"Divination?" He whirled in triumph, gesturing to the line of unwashed tea cups on her counter, dark eyebrows arched in waiting, and she heated. "Tasseomancy?"

She had got the idea in her head after her last visit to Aza-thé, that perhaps reading tea leaves might be the specialty she had been searching for.

When she had entered the tearoom that day, Harper had hesitated at the host stand, taking a deep breath. The little cat meowed, leading her to a small table on the opposite end of the room from where she normally sat. There was no scroll in sight. Instead, Harper was obliged to use a small arrow marker to denote the time, date, and location of her birth. Her order would be based on her ascendant sign, her moon sign, and her sun sign. No other input was taken.

Once she had moved the arrow marker to the correct points, she had fidgeted in her seat. Her fingers itched to pull out her book, quieting her mind and losing herself in the familiar, but she decided that day she would try something new. Her focus instead shifted to the line of books beside her table. To her surprise, they were all on methods of divination. Tarot meaning journals, runic keys, a chart showing how to read bones. And there, just on the end of the shelf, a book on reading tea leaves. She pulled it out with interest, thumbing it open and quickly losing herself in the instructions.

When her tea cart rolled up to the table, it contained a dainty sampling of three different finger sandwiches — each representing her astrological signs — a steaming pot of black tea with peach and ginger and three individual teacups. Harper had looked up sharply, glancing around to see if the cart would be rolling on to deposit the cups elsewhere, but when it did not move, she realized they were all for her.

"To practice your tasseomancy."

The voice melted from the shadows once more, a ripple of black satin that shivered down her spine, and her thighs had tightened. Harper didn't know what it said about her that she was so turned on by merely a voice. A disembodied voice, no less. *What do you mean you don't know what it says? It means you're so horny you could crawl out of your skin.*

Depression, she had learned, was a fickle thing. It wrapped around her like a well-worn blanket most of the time, but on the rare occasions she was able to shake it off — like that afternoon in the tea shop — her other impulses flared to life, leaving her ravenous. If there had been a menu option to bend over the table and let that mellifluous, silky voice rail her into next week, she would have ordered two and a third to take home.

"Oh, um, thank you. That's perfect. I read tea leaves in one of my core classes, but it was a short section. For as much tea as I've been drinking, I'll be an expert in no time," she joked, unwilling to allow the voice in her head to remind her it would likely be one more thing at which she tried and failed.

"Well, we're thrilled to have you practice your craft beneath our roof," the voice had hummed, a note of amusement warming it. "Tea is more than hot water and some dried-out leaves. It's an elixir of health, and it reminds us to make time for simple joys. Nothing can rush a steeping leaf, and there is no problem that cannot be paused to enjoy a hot cup. Tea forces us to slow down and exist uninterrupted in a small moment. That's what's left at the bottom of your cup — the dregs of your problems. Reading the leaves will help you realize what you need to do to banish them from your life."

"That's a very good way of looking at it," she'd murmured, telling herself the heat she felt in her face was from the steaming tea cup and nothing more.

The shadowy voice was neither male nor female, only dark and sinuous, a whispering presence that comforted as much as it confounded. *Intelligent and kind and completely fuckable*. She was not attracted to people the same way her school friends had been. She needed to know the person first, be attracted to something about *them*, not merely the hormone-triggering idea of them, and regardless of what they may have looked like, the owner of the shadowy voice had captured her attraction. *What if they really are just the menu? Can you grind on a menu?*

"That's one of the reasons I like coming here," she continued after a moment, ordering herself to get it together. "To quiet my mind."

"Mmm, yes. It is a good place for that. Quieting our minds is one thing; better still to fill them with knowledge and compassion. Less room for despair. In any case, there's no vexation on either side of the veil that cannot be eased with a hot cup of tea and a good book. I'll let you get back to your studies."

Harper wasn't sure if she'd fully grasped the hang of reading the leaves yet, but it gave her something to practice in the evenings. She was going through an insane amount of tea, but at least she was hydrated.

Holt arched an eyebrow expectantly.

"Tea leaves," she admitted sheepishly. "But no, I haven't chosen a discipline yet."

"Divination is a very worthy area of study. One of the finest and most difficult. But be aware — heavy is the head that wears the laurel of knowing. With knowledge comes power, and with power comes responsibility."

"Did you just give me a superhero speech?"

"Responsibility," he went on peevishly, "inevitably leads to sacrifice. You must bear all at once, and it is a burdensome thing." His tone had grown somber, and his eyes seemed to glow.

"I don't think I have to worry about that because I'm not very good."

The cat man's laughter made the hairs on her neck stand out, as if his voice produced an electric charge. "There is plenty of time to learn if this is your chosen discipline. You'll also study cartomancy, scrying, pyromancy, a full range of techniques and skills. But you said you've *not* yet chosen your area of study. Why." It wasn't a question. The word was a challenge on his lips, and her spine straightened a bit.

"Um, that's–that's what I was saying. I–I wasn't asked to return to the Collegium this term. I missed a lot of classes and . . . I wasn't *invited to return*. But I hope to go back." She wasn't sure if it was true. As the words left her mouth, her stomach swooped, the very thought of the future — particularly her future as a witch — nearly leaving her breathless. "Um, maybe. Hopefully. But I'm not allowed to attend coven meetings until I do, so like I said. I don't know if I'm still a witch."

"A coven does not make a witch, little one. Dedication to the craft, service to sister and community, a lifetime of study — those are the things that matter. Not coven meetings and popularity contests. Those things don't matter at all."

"But you said the strength of the circle is what makes us strong," she shot back, fists balling, steak knife deposited, forgotten. "You literally *just* said that. That, without it," she deepened her voice to imitate his, ignoring his scowl as she did so, "'We're no different than ordinary humans.' And newsflash, asshole, some of us *don't* find strength in the sisterhood. Sometimes, the sisterhood is full of catty, mean girls. Sometimes it's just one more reminder that you're not good enough."

"The strength of a witch does reside in her coven alone," he countered, his voice steady, advancing on her again.

This time, Harper held her ground. *He'll have to knock you down to go through you.* "Like I said. That's not been my experience. And-and it's not just that. I flunked out of my classes. I wasn't welcomed back. If I can't study, I don't see how I can ever be an accredited member of the coven."

"*Particu*larly," he went on, ignoring her as if she'd not spoken, "when one's coven is run to serve singular egos, and not the unity of the whole. Do you think every witch beneath the moon is privileged enough to attend a specific, private school for study? There have been witches forever, but I assure you, the Collegium concept is quite new, all things considered. Rather, it is the strength of a sisterhood that transcends time and place that makes us strong. We all serve under the same moon, Harper Hollingsworth, whether you are a solitary witch or one with a large coven. Whether self-taught or under the guiding hand of a teacher."

"Did you just steal my name with your creepy cat magic?"

"It's actually all over your mail," Holt sniffed, gesturing to the table. "Recycling is free, you know. The coven here is a perfect example. Ego. Blind ambition. Closed hands instead of open arms for a fellow witch. No respect for the ties that bind us all. You're not missing anything by not attending their meetings. That's a mark on them, not on you. Understand?"

She nodded, hesitantly. His voice had grown sharp, but the edge of it was not directed at her. *Mom and her friends.* Suddenly, she wanted to tell this annoyingly handsome cat everything, every word uttered at tea that day and Ilea's cryptic comments after, every professor she'd ever had who played favorites amongst the students, every junior coven meeting that seemed designed to exclude, instead of fostering the bond of sisterhood.

"You have no idea what it's like out there. Almost every coven meeting I've ever attended has been a popularity contest, and that doesn't end at school."

"I know what it's like. And a large part of that is simply human nature, I'm afraid. Young women taught to compete with each other at an age when hormones and young adulthood are like a tidal wave. Unfortunately, there's very little chance of escaping it unless one is raised in a closed community. The true mark of a coven does rest in the junior ranks, but in its leadership."

"My mother had some friends over right after we moved here. They told her all about the high crone, how *dynamic* she is. Half the time, it sounded as if they were trying to talk themselves into believing she's so amazing, but none of them would say anything bad. They just danced around it."

"Because the culture she has created is one of control," he cut in, raking a bone-white hand through his thick hair. "This crone wants to be obeyed; she's not interested in fostering the coven of tomorrow. You know, the previous high crone used to say, 'We walk to the noose with our heads held high, for we do not walk alone.' *That* is the strength of a witch. It is only when she forgets her sisters and her calling that our work is corrupted. You are young on your path and heavy with grief. You only need to find a coven who will nurture the witch you are, not demand you conform to their standards. Do you understand? The time is coming, Harper Hollingsworth. I swear it."

Harper wasn't sure if she did, but she felt breathless and overwhelmed by his words, the vehemence in his tone, and the green fire in his eyes. She wondered if *this* was the point of a familiar, for she could never remember a single time in all her life when Ilea had inspired her to *be* a witch.

"Do you live with your witch?" She wasn't sure why she was asking. *What are you going to do if he says no, invite him to stay? Get him a little bed, let him and Ilea have catfights in the driveway?*

Holt flinched at the question, suddenly very interested in the meager contents of her freezer. "I don't have a witch at the moment, actually." His voice, so full of passion just a few seconds earlier, was suddenly disinterested. *That's a typical deflecting cat.*

"But I thought you said you went to the Collegium?"

"Oh, I did," he agreed with a shrug. "But that was many years ago, long before you were even born."

She swallowed at the reminder that his appearance was nothing more than an assumed glamour, like slipping on a borrowed skin. "I thought familiars had to be reassigned if they're surrendered."

"I wasn't sur*ren*dered!"

"Then what happened to your witch?"

His head lifted, meeting her eye. "She died."

Harper felt his unexpected words like a physical blow, hunching slightly as they caught beneath her ribs, making contact with the yawning emptiness inside her.

"She died, and then I was *reassigned*." His voice was mutinous, his glare lethal. "And then *that* witch decided to leave the craft altogether."

"That seems enormously unlucky," she murmured weakly.

"Yes, well, I'm a black cat through and through."

"And–and you've not been sent to a new witch since?"

Holt shrugged noncommittally, and the gesture was so en*tire*ly feline that Harper half expected him to swish a tail. "It's entirely possible I misfiled the paperwork, slowing down the process. But I don't especially want to be reassigned, not yet."

She wondered what his witch had been like. She wondered if he mourned her loss, if his type could even feel things that deeply. She didn't know how old Ilea was, just like she didn't know how old the cat before her might be, but they were old, decades older than they looked, and surely a creature that long livèd would not care for something as petty as a mere witch's lifespan.

"Your Aunt Pernella," he began suddenly, redirecting the conversation, "despite what lies you may have been told, was a daring witch with a brilliant mind for charm casting and the most impressive library of spellbooks I've ever seen. She had been collecting since childhood. Grimoires, field guides, ancient spell scrolls . . . It was all in her workroom, right down in the —" He turned to her reading nook, frowning at the chintz floral wallpaper. "Right down in the cellar . . . which you've *drywalled* over?" He spun, sputtering in outrage. He glared at her, lip curling, and Harper was tempted to renew her resolve to stab him in the eyeball. "Why would you do such a thing?!"

"I just moved in!" she yelped, brandishing the steak knife again in warning, huffing when he rolled his eyes. "I didn't even know there was a cellar! Do you think the books are still there?"

She wasn't sure when she'd grown so recklessly stupid. *Why are you asking his opinion?! He's probably a scam artist. He read your mail and looked you up online, that's how he knows about Aunt Pernella. He's probably three minutes away from pulling out one of your frying pans to bash your skull in.*

"Oh, they're still here," Holt breezed confidently, breathing deeply. "The whole place still smells exactly the same. It means they're being kept safe, in any case. If you ever want to remodel, please let me know before you get rid of anything, I'll take the whole lot off your hands for a very good price."

As if to punctuate his words, he taped his long, black lacquered claws against the countertop, and Harper frowned. She *knew* those claws, but couldn't place how.

"Why don't you want to be reassigned? Are you tired of working with witches? Are you collecting imp unemployment or something?" *Do you want to be my familiar and teach me how to witch? It comes with the bonus of terrorizing Ilea.*

"I'm waiting for someone," he admitted slowly, not deigning to answer the entire question. His head snapped to the right, as if something had caught his attention, and Harper wondered if she had a mouse problem. "Someone in particular. She doesn't think she wants a familiar."

"Maybe she's not a cat person. Is that, like, extremely insulting?"

"It's not," he laughed. "She does not have need of me right now . . . but she will. Someday soon, she will need me. She will need all the help I can give her. And I do not wish to be bound to another when that day comes."

Silence hung between them for a moment, weighted by their individual thoughts. "Do you miss her?" The words seemed to leave her in an unconscious blurt, and her face heated again. "I-I mean your witch. The one who died."

Another long, heavy pause. Harper didn't know why, but she felt possessed by the desire to tell this strange man her entire life story, tell him every excruciating detail of the last two years, how broken and worthless she felt, how empty she felt inside. She wanted to tell him that somewhere on the street behind her cottage, one of the neighbors burned a fire almost nightly. Smoke drifted on the balmy late-summer air, and the breeze carried the smell of it to her open windows, wrapping her in a haze of familiarity as she drifted to sleep, the only time she was able to sleep restfully, even though she slept all the time.

"My sort isn't meant to be distracted by human concepts like time," he said at last. "The time you spend on this place of existence is negligible, I'm afraid to say. What is the life of one witch to the root of the sisterhood itself? We're not meant to count days and weeks and years as your kind does. A day in the life of a witch is barely a minute to the familiar at her side. A week is barely an hour. A year, no more than a day."

Harper swallowed down everything she'd wanted to blurt. She had no kinship with this strange, enigmatic cat-man, no more than she had ever had with the familiar who dwelled beneath her mother's roof, who would have gladly suffocated her in her cradle if they'd ever had half the chance. She was bobbing on a solitary sea, and there was no one who understood. She wanted him to leave, she decided, her throat feeling thick. She wanted to be left alone with her grief, as she always was.

Holt spun, his unnatural green eyes glossy and vibrant. "But not a day passes when I do not think of her. She was an exceptional, *singular* witch, and more than that, she was the most giving person I've ever known. She overflowed with kindness, kindness and sacrifice. I will mourn her loss long after there is anyone else left alive who will remember her name. There are some things that transcend what we are, child. We all walk beneath the same moon, and grief is eternal. So yes, I miss her a great deal."

She turned away and hunched again, squeezing her eyes against the pain. There was a sob brewing in her throat, and if she tried to speak, she would not be able to hold it in. *If grief is eternal, why does it seem like I'm the only one suffering it?*

"Grief is the wound love leaves on our heart," he continued, again as if he could audibly hear her thoughts, and at that, she could not hold in the tears for another second.

Her sob came out in a strangled wheeze, but unlike everyone else in her life who acted as if her emotions were some hideous, embarrassing thing that she should feel shame over, Holt seemed unbothered.

"When does it stop hurting?" She was barely able to get the words out as her shoulders hitched, and that, too, didn't seem to bother the familiar.

"It doesn't."

He shrugged again, the very first time someone had told her there would be no end to the empty, ocean-like chasm within her. Every single person she had encountered over the last year and half had told the same pretty lie — that time would ease the ache inside her until it had vanished. This — this felt like the truth, at last.

"The strength of that ache is the tenacity of love, and it never fades." His voice, so full of vehemence just a short while ago, was now somber, gentled, but no less full of conviction. "What *does* happen, is that your heart will heal around it. Yes? It's not something that ever goes away, and like any bruise, to poke it will ache. But your heart will grow around it, protecting it, and it simply becomes a part of you. Don't ever expect that ache to go away, little one. But stop considering it a negative thing. Grief is a gift. Do you understand?"

It took her a long moment to answer, and she truly didn't know if she understood . . . but she wanted to try. *Grief is a gift*. If nothing else, it made more sense to her than *time heals all wounds*. "Yes . . . maybe."

"Maybe is good enough. Maybe is all we ever have. The truth of unknowable things is that they are forever unknowable. All we can do is study and take our strength where we can. *That* is the power of a witch."

It was the first time she could remember crying in front of another person without having someone hovering, attempting to quiet her. He seemed unperturbed as her shoulders shook, and if he'd been in his other form, she wouldn't have been surprised if he began grooming himself, heedless of her tears. She probably should have been embarrassed, she thought once she managed to get control of her emotions, but when she turned, Holt was across the room, rooting through her books.

"I wish I could have known her," she managed at last. "Your witch, I mean."

"Oh, you will." His voice was casual, and he took his time replacing the book he'd been holding on the shelf, his attention once more caught by something in the corner. He stared for a long moment, before turning to her at last. "You must learn what the darkness discovers, Harper Hollingsworth. You walk to the noose with your head held high, because you walk with *all* of your sisters beside you. *That* is the power of a witch."

When she walked him to what was apparently her back door, the object of his original quest was standing right there.

Harper took in Ilea as if for the first time. The form they took was just as haughty as they were in their feline skin — country club fashion, immaculate hair, and a disdainful air. Their lip curled back at the sight of Holt, but Harper thought she recognized a flash of panic.

"Ah, just the rat catcher I was looking for."

If what she had seen was indeed panic, they recovered quickly enough at Holt's words.

"What are you doing here?" Ilea demanded.

Harper scowled, instantly defensive. "He was visiting me. He's my guest. A better question is, what are *you* doing skulking around my door again?" As soon as the words were out of her mouth, she remembered the loose gravel strewn about the path. "Are you the one who was digging next to my door? You need to knock it the fuck off, Ilea. I already told you — you're not welcome here. My property begins at that line in the driveway. There is no reason for you to be beyond it."

Both of the familiars ignored her, staring each other down.

"It seems you have not registered your presence in town, kittling." Holt's voice was casual, but Harper could sense the trap there. Sheathed claws but ready to pounce.

"I haven't managed to find the time to make it all the way into the city," Ilea sniffed. "The coalition —"

"The coalition has very specific bylaws," Holt interrupted. "If you are an imp actively working in the vicinity, you are required to register your presence. To avoid doing so makes it look as if you are trying to hide something, Ilemauzer. I wonder what that could be?"

"I don't answer to you." Harper had heard Ilea's sneer a hundred million times before, but she had never before heard the slight edge of panic behind it. "For that matter, I don't know that I need to answer to the coalition either. I am bound to my witch, and the bylaws of her current coven state that no outside agency or organization is to supersede their doings. I think if you were to check statute number 487, you would find —"

"Do not speak to *me* of magical law." Holt's voice was a pitch-black hiss, advancing on Ilea in a way that made the other familiar gulp.

Harper felt frozen in place, her heart hammering and the tiny hairs at the back of her neck standing on end, watching the two cats parley. If she thought she'd witnessed the evidence of Holt's power in her little cottage, she realized now that what she'd seen was a mere suggestion. The very air around him seemed to ripple, and his eyes were a green inferno. The only power she had ever seen from Ilea was in their poisonous tongue. *A commonplace talent, comparatively.*

"I am older than you, kittling." Holt's face was mere inches from Ilea's, his voice a menacing whisper, silky like black satin. "I was there, dancing before the fires when the old ways were first forged. I was there to be named by the first witch who claimed an imp. Do not presume to tell me *any*thing."

Holt stepped back, opening his arms wide, and the fraught moment was broken. "Do not think that the actions of this high crone have gone unnoticed by the coalition. This coven is poisoned, rotten from the root." A swift glance back to

Harper, accompanied by a sharp-edged smile. "Consider yourself lucky to not be one of their numbers, lovely girl."

Ilea stiffened when Holt turned to them once more, but the supernatural chill that had rippled around him for several moments had thawed.

"Do not get comfortable, kittling. Their time is nearly at its end. Now be gone with you. Let's see if you can get to the office to register before I make it there to report you."

He backed them into the cottage, slamming the door shut on her mother's familiar, whirling on Harper as soon as they were alone once more.

"You mentioned something about your door? Do you think they're trying to break in?"

She swallowed hard, attempting to marshal her spinning thoughts. "Um, when I got home a week or two ago, there was loose gravel in front of the door. I thought maybe an animal was digging in the rocks."

"Or an animal jumping from your window sill into the rocks."

She sputtered in outrage at the thought of Ilea's fluffy white form peering into her window. "*Fucking* Ilea! There was another time, right after we moved in. Like, the same day. I opened the door, and they were standing on the stoop, stretching."

"Stretching?"

She closed her eyes, attempting to envision the way Ilea had been stretched up against the doorframe, gasping when she realized what they were doing. "When I was little, we used to keep a key on the top ledge of the door, just in case Morgan and I ever got locked out after school." She gasped again, slapping a hand over her mouth. "Do you think — do you think they're after the books in the cellar? Are there rare, valuable spellbooks down there?" She began to pace, caught up in the story writing itself in her head. "Maybe Ilea is working for the high crone! The coven is going to try and work some dark magic that's only in one of Aunt Pernella's grimoires, or maybe —"

She cut off when she realized he was laughing at her.

"Wow, calm down, Nancy Drew. You went from, like, zero to sixty on that."

Harper scowled as Holt continued to chuckle.

"Everything of value was moved already. The books are still there, it's true, but some extremely rare ritual tools, recipes, and spells Pernella crafted over the years were gifted before her death. They're all safe at the Brackenbridge house, and there is literally no safer place in this town or any other. I would love to see Ilea attempt to break in there. Actually, that would be a fun thing to organize. That's a *good* idea . . ."

She huffed, and he shrugged off the thought, turning to her with a smile.

"But you're right. Ilea likely does not know that. What I can promise you is they're not smart enough for subterfuge. If they think you have anything of value, they'll be looking to sell it on the black market. Bad news for them, because I *am* the black market. Take heart, little one. There will be a new coven coming soon. It might cause some tension with your family, but you will find the place where you belong, and a circle of sisters to welcome you. *That* is the power of a witch."

He exited through the same door upon which he had entered, nearly two hours ago, Harper realized. She had been attending the junior coven since childhood, had gathered herbs and practiced charms, completed her core competencies at the Collegium, and sat in a circle every week, shoulder to shoulder with those of her kind. It was ironic, she thought, that the last two hours were the first time in her life she'd ever *felt* like a witch.

She hoped, wherever he was, that her father was laughing at the amusement of it all . . . and that her grandmother had heard the black cat that was currently trotting through the garden, his tail in the air, calling her a commonplace talent.

Chapter 6

O *OTD: crushed velvet slip dress over sheer Swiss dot blouse. Fishnets with ruffled ankle socks. Lug sole Mary Janes. Oversized cable knit cardigan.*

Harper sucked in a low, slow breath. The table was beautiful. A dark stained walnut, inlaid with gold. It depicted the moon cycle along the top edge, with signs of the zodiac lining each side. She read over the instructions again, knowing she couldn't procrastinate any longer.

Shuffle your deck, cut from the center. Remove three cards & place in the spread. Once the cards are placed, do not disturb them. Return the deck to the box, face down.

The inlaid template was a simple three-card spread. Past, present, and future. It was the first time the little cat had led her to one of the tarot tables, and she didn't know why the notion of having her cards read in order to inform her tea selection had her heart thumping in her chest. At the top of the table was a gold filigree basket, just large enough to hold the narrow deck. Harper exhaled steadily. *Now or never.*

Shuffle the deck, cut from the center.

She shuffled the cards, twisting them this way and that at regular intervals, being no stranger to a tarot deck. She could list each of the Major Arcana on sight and a handful of properties relating to each card and knew the rudimentary basics of the Minor Arcana, but she was no tarot reader. Divination had not been of particular interest to her mother, and so she and Morgan had not grown up in a household with regular instruction.

The divination section of her core competencies had been glossed over by the instructor, and as a result, Harper was more likely to examine her makeup in a scrying ball than she was to see a glimmer of the future yet to pass. Tarot cards were pretty illustrations and little more, but it was obvious that her shadowy tea host placed more stock into the cards than anyone in her family.

Remove three cards and place them in the spread.

The first card she pulled from the deck depicted the solitary figure shrouded in black. Before them, four golden cups lay on their sides, their blue liquid contents spilled along the bottom edge of the card. The figure's eyes were closed, the sky above them dark and stormy, and the tears that ran down their cheeks held the same pattern as the spilled liquid at their feet, caught in the 5th cup.

Well, fuck. That's a great start.

The second card showed six cups. Harper blew out an exasperated broth, already annoyed with her subconscious. Six scattered cups on a bright emerald field beneath the glorious sun. Upon the card, two children played, and a stylized flower grew from each of the cups. It seemed like a happy card. Or at least, it would have been if it were upright. She placed the reversed Six of Cups in the center space on the template, sucking in another deep breath.

You only have one chance left. Don't blow it. When her third and final card proved to be the Seven of Cups, Harper nearly flipped the table over in frustration. *You had one job.*

She didn't know why she expected her broken brain to obey her that day, when it had never done so in the past. Her father was the one who'd pushed when she was a moody adolescent, claiming something wasn't right, that she wasn't acting like herself, in a way that seemed more than typical preteen angst. Even then, Harper thought with a snort, her mother had simply assumed she was being difficult and lazy. She had a feeling her mother had been mortified at her eldest daughter's diagnosis of clinical depression, but she had liked her therapist, and for a time, it seemed as if she was better.

The family therapist she'd seen as a teen had retired from practice when she'd still been in undergrad, and there had been no professional intervention in her life since then. *And now look at you. The whole suit of cups, just yeeting all your trauma onto the table in public. Great. Excellent. That's not mortifying or anything.*

The tea shop was quiet, but she knew it wouldn't be long before it was bustling, as it always was mid-week. Soon, they would be too busy to hover over her, but for now, she had the proprietor at her singular disposal, and Harper knew it would only be a few minutes before they slid up to her table to inspect her spread.

"Oh my."

Harper jumped at the voice coming from over her ear, covering her face with her hands as they gazed down at her cards. "I know. It's mortifying."

"I wouldn't go that far, sweet one, but it certainly tells a story."

"Yes, one of emotional dysregulation," she mumbled, looking down at her hands so they wouldn't see the way her cheeks heated. *Sweet one!*

"One of emotional fatigue," they corrected, "and it is hardly surprising, given the recent stress you have experienced. The Five of Cups—"

"Grief," she nodded. "I know that one."

"Grief and loss," they agreed, their voice shifting to her side. "Self-explanatory, I suppose. But also self-pity. Stasis. Being trapped in a cycle of unending grief and pity. And let's give credit where it is due, sweet one, because that card shows your past."

"I'm not sure if the present is much better. Although, I don't think I know the full meaning of this one reversed."

They rumbled beside her, a low croon of amusement, and she nearly levitated off her seat. It was ridiculous to have a crush on the voice, she reminded herself for at least the hundredth time that week, but Harper couldn't help it.

"I think what is most amusing about the placement of this card is the utter plethora of meanings it could potentially hold for your present circumstances," they chuckled warmly. "This is a card of nostalgia, of happy childhood memories, of passing things down from one generation to the next. It is a card of homecoming. Reversed, its meaning is not so different. It is still a card of homecoming, although perhaps for unhappier reasons. Homecoming along with the realization that one can never truly go home again, for the home of your childhood no longer exists, for you are no longer a child."

"Nothing will ever feel like home again," she agreed in a near whisper.

"It is good to remember those happy memories of our past, but it does not do to dwell within them. The passing of traditions down in the upright card in the reverse might be tainted with unwanted obligation. The realization that the path set out for you in childhood may not be the one you are meant to follow. Breaking the bonds of family to forge one's own future. You see, my sweet one, we can basically take our pick."

At that, Harper burst out laughing. Her shadowy host knew most of her story at that point. They did not linger long at her table each time she visited, but they *did* linger. *Longer than they do at anyone else's table.*

She had noticed, several weeks earlier, that while the tea shop varied in its business, the patrons who sat to enjoy their lunch did so without the complement of conversation from their host. She had never before seen another guest talking to the empty corner of their table, had never seen any of them being given instruction on which book to select for the day, had never overheard anyone talking about themselves, answering the perceptive and prescient questions asked by the shadows. They only talked to her, and she relished the singular attention.

After that first disclosure of her father's death, they asked about where she lived. How long had she lived there, and what prompted her family's move to Cambric Creek? The fluffy, paranormal romance she'd picked off the shelf had been paired with a warm, spicy cinnamon chai, and each sip was balmy and comfortable, a perfect counterpoint to the autumn backdrop of the story.

They asked if she was a student at the university as they topped off the hot water for her lovely citrus-rose blend, the pairing chosen for a book of non-Euclidean poetry. They were surprised to hear she had completed her under-graduate degree several years earlier, lightly quipping that they were a terrible judge of age when it came to humans.

Harper's eyes would follow where she perceived them to be, convinced she was able to pick out a weight to the shadows, a slightly deeper tone in the darkness, owing to the fact that she was an expert at matching blacks, she thought with pride.

"I don't know, I think it's all of them," she laughed, her mortification over the initial card draw dissipating. She should've known better. This was one of the only places in the world where she didn't need to mask her true self, for the shadows never seemed to care.

"It may well be. But I think it's useful to be aware of each. You will always have your happy memories, my sweet one, but you cannot live in the past. Others may be disap-pointed in the path you forge for yourself, but you must remember that their disappointment belongs to them and them alone. It is not yours to manage. And perhaps you may even find a way to incorporate those passed-on tradi-tions into your future, but it cannot be someone else who dictates it."

"And the Seven? The future card?" Her voice was cautious, and Harper bit her lip, anticipating what they would say.

"The most auspicious card of all, sweet. You see the different paths spilling from each cup? Those are the possibilities before you. It is good to be a dreamer, but one must remember that action is required to achieve those dreams. All in all, this is quite a well-threaded spread."

Harper's eye was drawn back to the past card, something invisible catching her attention, a ripple she saw from the corner of her eye, even though nothing was there.

"Unhappiness and grief. Trapped in a cycle of misery. Unable to move forward. And that is in the past now."

The same ripple of the air, and her eyes moved to the center card. Harper liked to think that she was following their hand.

"Homecoming and memories. The knowledge that what others want for you may not be what you need to do for yourself. Only you can pick the road before you. And here — all of the possibilities for that road."

She thought of all of her imagined futures, all of the jobs she might take and places she might live. *Action is required to achieve those dreams.*

"I find this to be a most optimistic spread. You are ruled by your emotional center in your heart, my sweet one. That is not something to be ashamed of. It would have been far stranger to find a spread of pentacles before you. Now, for your book . . . Nonfiction, I think, for today. If you go over to the astrological chart table in the front corner, you'll find a pinned blue morpho butterfly. Ethically sourced, of course. On the small shelf beside it, you will find a series of textbooks, all numbered on the spine. I believe number three is the one we want."

Harper grinned as she pulled the textbook from the shelf, as directed. *Emotional Display, Regulation, and Burnout: Understanding the Suit of Cups.*

"Good girl. We're going to turn you into a prognosticator yet. I'm going to start your tea. Happy reading."

She bit her lip again at the endearment, letting her thighs drop open a fraction beneath the table. If a shadow moved between her open legs to tickle at the front of her panties, she would've had no complaints. *Fuck me and call me a good girl. I'm a simple girl with simple needs.*

Harper had never understood how anyone could be attracted to a collection of parts first and the person operating them second. It didn't matter how attractive society told her someone was — until she got to know them, a tumbleweed had a better chance of falling out of her dress than her libido kicking into overdrive because of someone's abs.

She had seen her sister's big dicked lacrosse crush on social media, Morgan taking her through a series of photos, and Harper could objectively agree that the young man was handsome in the way conventionally attractive people always were. He had arms and legs and an eighteen-year-old's washboard stomach, a nice smile, and — as her sister pointed out in a multitude of photos — a prominent bulge at his groin. *A collection of parts*. She had made all of the appropriate noises and agreements until Morgan was mollified, as a good sister should. She still didn't understand it though. *He has a very upright skeleton! She has a complete set of teeth! They have the correct number of fingers, well done!*

Attraction to parts didn't make any sense to her brain, but attraction to *this* sinuous, curling voice? Their kindness and knowledge? Their ability to brew a perfect cup of tea? She didn't know if they possessed arms or wings or tentacles, if they walked upright on two legs, or if they had legs at all.

Harper had no idea what parts they possessed, but whatever they were, she was certain they could make her scream in pleasure, for she was already crushing hard.

When the tea cart rolled out, it made several stops around the room, attending to each of the patrons who'd come in since her tarot reading. None of them, she could tell, were spoken to.

"An earthy yerba mate, enhanced with fragrant pink strawberries, dark cocoa nibs, and pink peppercorn for a bit of heat through the sweetness. Grounded, with brightness to counter the dark and spice to counter the sweet. Balance in all things, sweet one. Enjoy."

"Thank you," Harper whispered, arching in her seat like a cat at the phantom weight of a hand at the back of her neck.

Attraction parts seemed like a silly thing, but attraction to *this*? It made perfect sense to her. *And if someone doesn't understand, that's not your problem to manage either.*

Chapter 7

O *OTD: Unstructured maxi dress with moth-wing shawl, flats that are probably going to only be comfortable for three minutes, jeweled ear cuff.*

They moved exclusively through the shadows. The shop's windows were long and high, and the stacks of books and cases of curiosities were placed in a way that allowed the light to bounce off them all across the shop, casting long shadows for the shadowy host to traverse. She didn't know *what* they were, but the shadows were a necessity.

The first time she'd realized they needed the shadows to move had been the afternoon a section of the dining room was closed off. What had started off as a dreary late morning when she'd left the house had swelled into a monsoon by the mid-afternoon, thunder shaking the building as the rain pelted down, the sky a uniform wall of dark grey cumulonimbus botting out any hope the sun might yet make an appearance that day. Hope for other people, of course. She was thrilled with the unexpected deluge, content to sit in her little nook and drink tea while the thunder rumbled all afternoon.

"Why do I get the impression this weather suits you," they'd accused, sliding up to her table after the tea cart had made its mysterious circuit of the room, depositing plates and steaming pots to the handful of other patrons.

She grinned at the corner. A half shade darker, likely imperceptible to most people, but when your entire wardrobe was black, the differences between *coal* and *raven* and *tar* were unmistakable. "You're not wrong," she'd agreed with a laugh. "I love weather like this. Perfect for reading."

Several candelabras had been lit around the bulk of the dining room, but the back of the room, where it opened into the glassed-roof solarium, was cordoned off. The flickering candle flames cast bouncing shadows all around the room, but the back of the room was uniform in its dimness. *Shadows. They don't need darkness. Only shadows.*

Now she knew where to look. Harper liked to imagine that they were sitting across from her, enjoying savories and scones, sipping hot tea instead of leaving her alone . . . until she realized she knew nothing about them. *How rude. They ask after you all the time. They know about your home life and mental state, your degree; they know you're a witch. You don't even know what they are!*

She got her opportunity the very next day. Storms were in the forecast once more, and she arrived to find even more of the dining room cordoned off.

"Do you ever close on days like this?" she asked once they slid up to her table. "If there's not enough light for the shadows?"

For several long, echoing moments, her question received silence in response. Harper had the impression she'd taken them by surprise. They normally spoke first, but today, she had been watching. The candelabras were lit again, and in the wavering shadows they threw across the floor, she had watched a shiver pass through them. Normally, the long shadows from the high windows were stable and straight. By contrast, the flickering candlelight produced a wibbly, wobbly surface for them to traverse, and it seemed to her as if they needed to shift back and forth repeatedly just to make it to her small table.

"I had considered it today, now that you mention it. But I'm very glad to see you all the same."

She laughed at the careful response. "The pleasure is mine. Always. But if this is too much trouble, I promise you won't hurt my feelings if you tell me to leave."

They tutted in response. "If worse comes to worse, there are lights I can turn on. Are you practicing your cards today?"

When she told them about her desire to study divination a bit more seriously, they leapt upon the opportunity to instruct her with zeal. Every visit to the tea shop involved a tarot reading, and she was not allowed to leave until she read the dregs of her cup. Harper couldn't say that she had improved her skill at either discipline, but she was enjoying these lessons more than she'd ever enjoyed a single day of classes in school.

"I am. I already have a deck ready to go."

"Very good. And what are you reading today?"

She grinned. She hoped there would never be another eatery where *what are you reading today* was the chief method of placing an order. Closing the book open on the table before her, she showed them the cover. It was one they had picked out for her several visits earlier, and she was taking her time getting through it. The illustration depicted a stormy sky and roiling sea, an eldritch mass of tentacles and eyes looming in the surf, and a little girl standing at the water's edge.

The shadows purred thoughtfully in contemplation. "Which part?"

"The girl just came back to the house at the shore as an adult."

"Hmmm . . . wistful nostalgia. The bittersweet certainty that things can never be as they once were."

"The Six of Cups."

"Exactly, sweet one, exactly. Good girl. I know just the tea."

Harper felt the precise moment when they left the table, the little nook seeming somewhat brighter, even as the air took on a flat quality, the absence of their crackling energy nearly tangible.

The toneless groan of the shop's bell sounded just then, a couple stepping through the doorway. She watched the little cat leap from its cushion, hurriedly greeting the newcomers before attempting to herd them down the aisle to one of the tables with the scrolls.

"Look, it wants us to follow it. How cute!"

Harper hid her laughter in her napkin when the cat yowled in frustration, glaring at the befuddled couple as they continued to loiter about the entrance before turning to where she sat with an exasperated shake of its whiskers. *Just think — you were that clueless, too, in the beginning.*

"Looks like you're going to have your hands full today," she murmured when the tea cart made a jerking journey to her table, gesturing with her chin to the table of newcomers who were now puzzling over the spirit board.

"I do believe you are correct," they sighed, and Harper took the opportunity to nudge out to the second chair at her table with her toe. "Promise me you're going to come sit down for a moment when they leave. I'm exhausted just watching you try to get the tea cart across the room. I can't imagine how you're feeling."

Another long pause. She had a feeling they found her ability to track them through the shadows disconcerting.

"If it were anyone else asking me, I would simply pretend I was already gone. This is white tea with vanilla and pear, and a vanilla madeleine."

She burst out laughing as they left the table in truth, and a moment later, a low light was lit. A nightlight, she thought, from its placement close to the floor. One by one, they clicked on, three of them in total, creating long, familiar shadows across the floor. She understood why they did not keep them lit under normal circumstances – it did dampen the overall effect of the tearoom's aesthetic, but she couldn't imagine they would be able to serve another table simply using the flickering flames of the candles as their guide.

The first sip of her tea tasted oddly old-fashioned. As she sipped again, Harper felt nostalgic for drawing rooms and doily-covered furniture and creaking old floors, the sounds of childhood. The third sip had a tinge of melancholy, and on the fourth, she reopened her book.

As the girl in the pages moved through the rooms of the home she'd known as a child, tears pricked at her eyes. The girl had lived through something fantastical and traumatic, something that had shaped the woman she became, yet for all her Eldritch adventures, the house was just a house, despite all of the things that had happened there in the preceding chapters. The rooms were just empty wooden boxes, the time spent playing there lost to the wind, and with each sip of the tea, she felt her heart grow heavier. Nothing would ever feel like home again, and she wondered if that too, was an eternal emotion shared by all, regardless of age or species.

"What do you think?"

She jumped, lost in her reverie, as they approached the table. She realized with a start that the other couple was gone already.

"Sit."

Their chuckle was like the crinkle of tissue paper close to the back of her neck, making her shiver. When she was able to discern the barest darkening of the shadow across the table, she was mollified.

"The tea was perfect. I wouldn't have tried that one on my own. I don't know how you managed to brew something that tastes nostalgic. Do you think it's a universal experience? The Six of Cups? The reality that home will never be home again?"

"I think," they hummed after a moment, the melliflu-ous glide of it seeming to creep over her skin, "that most emotional responses are rooted in universal experience for most."

"My mom sold our house after my dad died." She tipped back her teacup, draining it to the dregs. "I'll never forget how it felt walking through it for the last time. Everything was empty. There was no sign that anyone had lived there, or cried there, or that children had been raised there. There was nothing left of him. There was nothing left of any of us. It was like a collection of cardboard boxes all taped together. It was never going to be home again. I know exactly how the girl in the book feels."

"I think most of your kind can empathize with that emotion, my sweet one. Coming home after your first taste of adult freedom and being restrained by parents who still seek to treat you as a child. Coming back to the place you once lived after a death or divorce or some other cataclysmic event that has profoundly shaped your life. Coming back to a place after you built your own existence far away from it . . . In this regard, I think you are right. The Six of Cups is universal."

Harper nodded vehemently, wiping at her eyes.

"But consider—are not all the cards universal in their own way? Each of you will wear the noose of the Hanged Man at some point in your life. Sacrifice, stagnation. Everyone will face the temptation of the Devil card. Materialism, addiction, and lust. You all experience the disharmony of the lightning-struck Tower. But so, too, do you experience the overflowing joy of the Ten of Cups. The Tower reversed, harmony restored. The wisdom and rigidity of the Hierophant and the bliss of the Lovers. Death is the ultimate unifier — a beginning and an end at once. All of these are universal experiences. The cards merely offer guidance and awareness.

And if all of these are universal emotions and experiences, it seems to me that you are far too hard on yourself, sweet."

Harper choked out another laugh, using her sleeve to pat her cheeks dry. "I guess. What about you? Are they universal experiences for you as well?"

Once more, they took their time in answering. "I am a watcher of others. And does that not still count? If I am here to watch you experience sorrow and joy, does not a bit of that sorrow and joy become my own, having experienced it through you?"

"That is entirely too deep for me," she protested laughingly. "Don't you know I flunked out of school?"

A ripple of black satin wrapped around her shoulders as they laughed with her.

"This is why I like tea. There is no other beverage in the world that can so thoroughly conjure emotion. Today we brewed a pot of nostalgia, but tomorrow perhaps something to energize, to ignite the senses and provide creative inspiration. The day after that, it might be the same brew you were served as a sick child, reminding you of maternal care. Again, you are too hard on yourself. I've scarcely known another human with your aptitude and love for learning."

"Maybe you're just a very good teacher. You know," she hesitated, biting her lip, "I don't even know your name."

She had given the topic a fair amount of thought already.

There was nothing quite as powerful as a name. As a lover of books and of languages, she especially knew that to be true — all words had meaning and importance, but names held a particular importance. A name gave the impermanent permanence, the overlooked some sense of remembrance. To have a name was to be *seen*, even for the briefest of moments, is proof of one's incontestable existence. Knowing the name of another was a gift, a way to acknowledge them, to call them into account, regardless of how casually people treated introductions. She had read enough stories over the years, after all, of faeries and goblins and demons alike — they jealously guarded their names, for names held power.

It had occurred to her some weeks back that she was unaware of her shadowy crush's name, and once the thought had taken root in her mind, it was impossible to think of anything else. Harper wondered about their native tongue as she stared out the window on the trolley each day, considered that their name might be in some unknown language, older than the archaic Sumerian texts currently stacked on her coffee table, paged through each evening, looking for a name that fit.

"A name," they mused slowly, as if the concept was one they had never considered.

"A name? The thing people use to call you? Your personal label?"

"My sort have little use for such things," they admitted for a moment. "We exist on the cusp of this world and the other, in the shadows. There are very few who even know of our existence. As I said, I am a watcher. I am a bit of an outlier for communing so closely with the topside world, but I find the individuals who come through these doors fascinating. But there is no need for a name when one is unseen. As it is, I am a bit befuddled at how you are able to address my voice with such precise placement. I have never known a human who is able to see one of my kind."

"Well, there you go. I'm not just a human. I'm a witch." It felt good saying it. It may have been silly, but Harper was sure that somewhere, Holt would have been proud of her.

"Even still. You have addressed my voice correctly from the beginning. You managed to deduce that I move through the shadows without being told."

"I wear black every single day. I can see the different shades and tones. It's really not that hard when you know what you're looking for."

"Quite frankly, I don't ever want to hear about you flunking out of school again."

She laughed again, mollified by the way the darkness across the table seemed to shiver.

"Do you take a physical form?"

"I can assume whatever form is required. Regrettably, though, I spend so little time topside that I cannot hold it for very long."

"Whatever is required? What does that mean?"

In response to her question, the darkness coalesced before her, shadows unexpectedly taking form. One arm, then two, shifting like smoke and writhing like snakes, dense and black. A wing pulled from the black mass before dissipating. The arm reached up to the top of one of the spires of books above her head, plucking one from the stack. Harper felt frozen in her seat as the arm receded, dropping the book before dissipating back into the corner of the bookcase. She sat breathing hard, gripping the edge of the table tightly, feeling her pulse throbbing between her thighs. *Mark me down as scared AND horny. Like, so SO horny.*

The Devotion of the Volantines. It would be the next book she would read, she decided immediately.

"Maybe . . . maybe you just need to practice?" she breathed lightly, hoping her voice sounded calm. "What if I want you to ride the Ferris wheel with me at the Fall Festival? And you just vanish in the wind because you never practice holding your form? I could fall to my death."

"Presumably, you would be in the car holding on to the railing, so I don't see why my corporeal or incorporeal form would need to bear the brunt of guilt for you sliding out of your seat like a used napkin."

Her shoulders shook as she laughed, not expecting the biting humor, but delighted over it just the same. "Still. Ferris wheel. Fall Fest. You need to start preparing yourself."

"Are you not frightened?"

Their voice was guarded, and Harper gulped. She had the unshakable feeling the future of their odd relationship depended mightily on the rest of this conversation.

"What's there to be afraid of?" she asked finally. "Some shadows?"

"Most beings, I have learned, are afraid of what they do not know."

"I'm a witch," she countered steadily. "I must learn what the darkness discovers. And you are not unknown to me. You can practice your physical form with me anytime. But — I still don't know what to call you."

"Azathé is the only name I have ever chosen," they mused, "this tea shop is the only thing I have ever named."

"Is *that* what you want to be your name?" she asked dubiously.

"What?!" they huffed. "I think it's rather clever."

Harper threw up her hands in defense. She had no idea what it was that made the name allegedly clever, assuming it was an inside joke based on their own language and culture. "It's perfect then. Azathé it is."

The shadows rippled, and Harper imagined it was a show of pleasure.

"Is there no one else who talks to you?"

Once again, they took their time in answering. Harper wondered if they were uncomfortable being on the receiving end of questions about themselves. It was a reversal of roles, for they had been asking her pointed questions and teasing out the rest through tarot readings for months, and while she had never seen them talk to another patron during her visits, she thought they probably overheard plenty. *Between tarot draws and listening to conversations, they probably know the secrets of everyone in town.*

"I do not make a habit of making myself known," they answered carefully. "It dispels the mystique of the tearoom, for starters. As much I'm loath to admit it—"

"You're a gimmick," she finished, grinning hugely as they grumbled their assent.

"It's only rarely that I will speak to a guest, and only if I sense they require immediate intervention. Otherwise, I remain an invisible presence, and the vast majority of them are quite insensible to me."

She bit her lip, feeling rather sad for her shadowy friend. "That must be lonely for you. But wait, you talk to me."

"I do," they agreed, and she could sense the shadows shift-ing as the little cat brought in a new patron. "And you are enough."

"I'm not good company most of the time," she argued, but they cut her off, their voice right at her ear, and the nearness made her shiver in desire.

"You are *always* enough."

+ · · · + · · · + · · + · · · + · · · + · · · +

As she walked through the neighborhood that evening, she wondered what sort of form they would take before her — if they would have wings or arms, hooves like a beast, or if they would be a tentacled blob, like the creature in her book. *And does it matter?* It didn't, she decided. Arms and wings had pulled from their shape before they retrieved the book, but what they would settle on was anyone's guess.

When Morgan slapped on her back door that evening, Harper had a second spoon ready.

"Did you get into it with Ilea? I hope so. Please tell me you did. They have been spitting nails for *weeks*. I overheard

135

them today, mumbling about you conspiring with *suppressive persons*. Did you join Scientology? Are you, like, a government double agent? Please tell me you're having them deported to wherever it is familiars come from."

Harper laughed with her whole throat, the second time she had done so that day. It had been a good week.

"I'm not a double agent, and I'm not rich enough for Scientology. I did meet another familiar, though. He was over here, and he and Ilea got into it in the driveway. It sounds like Ilea is in the wrong with some paperwork and the other cat was going to snitch on them."

Morgan hooted. "That is the pettiest shit I've ever heard. It's giving big The Familiars of Cambric Creek vibes. I love it. 10 out of 10, would recommend to a friend."

They shared the pint of ice cream and companionable silence, watching the trashy reality show Harper had queued up on her laptop. It was nice. It was comfortable. It almost felt like home, she realized, understanding for the first time in that moment the full weight of the six of cups. Nothing would ever be *home* again, her childhood home. Even if they were still in the same house, her father was gone. He was never coming back, and his absence meant that home would never be home in the same way.

Grief is a gift. Perhaps this is what the familiar had meant when he said her heart would begin to heal around her grief.

Perhaps, eventually, this place would feel like home. A new home with her sister and her books and her tea house crush. It wasn't such a bad future to contemplate, Harper thought, remembering what Azathé had said about the seven of cups. Being a dreamer was well and good, but she would need to put in the work to bring her dreams to fruition.

She had always been a hard worker, despite her depressive episodes, and the thought of this future — a new home, her heart healed around the tender bruise of grief, her sister there to share a kind of full-fat ice cream, at least for another year or two, and her shadowy friend perhaps becoming more — was a future for which she was more than willing to put in the work. *And if nothing else, we always have the Fall Festival.*

Chapter 8

O OTD: *Floor-length lace duster, collared mini dress. Domino tights and batwing backpack.*

The book had looked completely innocent and inoffensive when they had placed it before her. *The Devotion of the Volantines*. A leather-bound volume from the nineteenth century, showing substantial wear, the plain cover gave her no hint as to what the pages held. The pages themselves were thin and the lettering small, forcing her to pay close attention as she read, which was not a hard chore.

Harper was certain her body was pulled as taut as a bowstring, her lip trapped between her teeth, and her hips canting invisibly beneath the table. She could pay attention to nothing but the book, and if the building caught fire while she was reading, that was how fire rescue would find her — tensely concentrating.

Every few pages, she would suck in a deep breath, reminding herself that they had *chosen* this book. It was an excellent selection. She was enjoying it quite a bit . . . but in all honesty, she would have preferred to be enjoying it in the privacy of her bed with a vibrator held to her clit, not rhythmically pulsing her thighs together in public, wishing her chair had a saddle horn she could grind against in her little nook between a cracked bell and a collection of cursed brooches.

A temple priestess giving herself in service, hardly an original archetype, Harper told herself, the jumping muscles in her thighs exciting the tingle between them. The priestess stripped bare before the altar, two of the lesser temple attendants anointing her with oil. There was probably a draft in the tearoom that day, she told herself as her nipples pebbled, the priestess on the page moaning in ecstasy as her attendants pinched her nipples to hardness, her oil-slickened breasts shining in the firelight. The priestess began her ritual, slicing a cut into her hand and letting it drip into a chalice. Behind her, the temple attendants began to pleasure each other, hips straddled, pelvis grinding, and Harper snapped shut the book.

It was impossible not to be reminded of the last time she'd been this publicly aroused and how *that* situation had played out.

Her study partner had been in several of her classes. They'd been in the library on campus late one evening, the building itself mostly empty and their upper floor completely deserted. Normally, being in the library alone had creeped her out, but *that* evening, the solitude had provided the perfect backdrop for their actions.

"This is making me so horny." It wasn't the first time the other girl had announced it. They were reviewing a chapter on sex magick and sustained pleasure, and Kel had informed Harper that she was turned on only a few minutes into their study session that night. "If they really want us to learn anything from this chapter, we'd be going down on each other as we read. I would pay to have someone lick my clit. Seriously, I'm so wet right now."

"Will you *stop*," Harper had protested laughingly. The subject matter on its own was not enough to arouse her, but she had always been suggestible, and the other girl's constant prattle over how horny she was had Harper squirming in her seat, panties drenched. "Do you have enough to pay someone to lick my clit too? Because you're making *me* horny."

The other girl had perked up. They continued to read. The silence only lasted a few more pages before the other girl, Kel, opened her legs, lifting her foot to the table. The gusset of her purple thong beneath her uniform skirt was soaked nearly black.

"Seriously, if we both have wet pussies, then why aren't we doing something about it? You lick me, and I'll lick you."

She had never been touched by another woman at that point. She'd covered her mouth to keep from gasping when

Kel dragged her hand up Harper's thigh, slipping a hand into her panties and stroking through her slick folds. The first touch of her tongue to the other girl's clit had Kel moaning, her eyes closed as she gave Harper instruction on where to lick and suck. When it was her turn, Harper was mortified over how fast she orgasmed against Kel's tongue, but as she was told afterward, "Don't worry, I lick pussy like a pro."

She'd wound up sitting on the edge of the table with Kel standing between her legs, rubbing their swollen clits together, grinding against each other. Their moans were soft and their pistoning hips provided a wet squelch where their bodies met, the knowledge that another student or professor might come up the staircase at any moment adding to the frenzy and heightening their arousal. Harper had come first, gripping the other girl's hips and bucking wildly against her, the slide of her clit against Kel's providing her enough friction to tip over the edge.

They'd had sex several times more that term, and it was never as good as it was in the library. Being in public now, reading about the soft moans of the temple attendants as they moved against each other in the same way she had, the priestess preparing to summon the dark god she served . . . it was too much. Harper escaped her table, making her way down the short hallway at the back of the dining room to the restroom. She could feel her heart thudding behind her lips, behind her eyes, between her thighs. The cold water she splashed on her face did little to cool the heat beneath her skin, but it was the best she could do.

When she returned to her table, she discovered her tea had been delivered. Azathé had not come by as she read, and at the time, Harper had assumed it was because the tearoom was crowded, but it was clear they had taken note of her reading material. *Well, they should. They picked it out.* A small card rested before the tray, listing the items contained therein — a black tea with satsuma and ginger. The fruity-spicy zing of it heated her cheeks at first sip, a clear complement to the spicier reading material before her.

The savories continued the trend — a ham and brie round, the meat crusted with black pepper, a phyllo cup of jalapeno-studded pimento cheese, and a sriracha-braised pork bun. The dessert was a decadent dark chocolate mousse, and Harper wondered how long they had been planning this menu. *Just waiting to spring the dirty books on you and feed you all the spicy food. Is this what heaven is like?*

The dining room had cleared out some. The large party of laughing goblins and trolls and orcs had left, some neighborhood get-together, she overheard. In their place were two older satyresses and the same green-haired girl who had been studying the very first time Harper had entered Azathé tearoom. The few tables on the other side of the parlor were the same groups that had been there before she had fled to the restroom and would likely be leaving soon.

Harper gazed around the room surreptitiously, trying to spot the waver in the shadows, the darker black shape moving through them, but when she was unable to spot them, she returned, almost reluctantly, to her book.

The dark god the priestess served was demon-like in appearance, with horns and wings, skin like stone, and garnet red eyes. She wondered if *their* physical form would be anything like this. Tail and wings, strong arms, and twisting horns. Despite what they thought, she wouldn't be afraid. On the contrary, the very thought flooded her core.

The beast was summoned by the priestess by laying herself out across the altar stone, supine and vulnerable, her oiled skin bare to the temple. The temple attendants were in a writhing frenzy behind her, pleasuring each other without heed, noisy in their lust, the priestess twisting against her stone plinth until her dark god appeared. Harper wondered if they would hold her down the same way, splaying her out before them, small and vulnerable.

The tribute the priestess paid for her demon god's summoning was with her body, Harper realized, biting her lip anew. Beneath the table, her thighs squeezed. There was an illustration on the following page in a woodcut art style, showing the priestess on her knees, bent over the altar stone as the demon godling rutted into her from behind. The woman's mouth was open in a cry, whether one of pain or pleasure, it was impossible to tell, for the demon behind her showed no restraint in the way he gripped her.

Harper wondered if *they* would be able to have her in such a way, fucking her harder and deeper than she ever had been before. Shadows did not exist on a gender binary, after all, and she was certain they had no secondary sex organs . . . but they said they could assume whatever form was needed. Does that mean two cocks like a naga? She bit her lip again, closing her eyes to envision the delicious memory of sliding her sex against another woman's. *They could do that. Or give you the biggest cock you've ever seen. Who knows what else they might be able to do.*

The temple attendants continued their frenzy, as the priest just paid homage to the one she worshiped – with her mouth, with her cunt, however the creature wanted to have her, over and over again. Harper was certain the stiffest breeze would immolate her, and when Azathé's dark, sinuous voice curled around her ear without warning, she yelped, sloshing her tea as she slammed the book shut.

"My sweet one, whatever is the matter? You are trembling like a newborn kitten. I only came to see how you are enjoying your pairing."

She was breathing hard, her chest heaving. Her face whipped to the side, where she sensed they were, and she knew the look on her face was positively mutinous. "The tea is delicious, thank you. I can tell much *thought* went into this pairing."

They hummed, a static-like sound that made goosebumps rise on her skin. "Only the best for you, sweetling. As always, your literature choices dictate the menu."

Harper choked out an incredulous laugh. "Ironic that you would call them *my* choices when the book was placed in front of me. But I do thank you for your excellent selection. I'm finding it quite instructive."

"Is that so? Well, I always think that no matter how esoteric the topic, there are applications and parallels that can be found in daily life."

"Oh, it's not so esoteric at all. I nearly felt as if this were autobiographical at a point. There was a section between the temple attendants that reminded me of my own university experiences. The illicitness, the public aspect of it . . . It's a shame you're so busy today. We could discuss our favorite parts, like our own private little book club."

Another burst of that static-like laughter, and then they left her, seeing to the other guests in the tearoom. Rather than emptying out, business remained steady, and at length, she accepted defeat. There would be no private audience that afternoon, but she did not begrudge them. She wanted her favorite tearoom to stay open and thrive, and she could not drink enough tea in her lifetime to make that happen alone. The little cat mewled at her as she left, checking out at the kiosk, not even getting a chance to say goodbye for the day.

When she got home, Harper wasted no time. It was not as satisfying as a partner, wasn't as spine-shivering as someone else's tongue, wasn't as toe-curling as being filled with a thick cock, and was hardly as exciting as scissoring in the Collegium library, but her fingers were reliable, and the suction cup on her dildo was strong. She had no idea which species the shape of the phallic silicone was meant to emulate — three joined spheres, growing larger towards the base, with a thick, ribbed underside – but it was better than the alternative.

The alternative, she was certain, meant marching into the tearoom and climbing atop one of the tables, presenting herself like the priestess to her demon, and Harper could not bear the potential rejection. Far better to take care of things at home, which she did, several times throughout the evening. She would slake the lust churning within her, clear her head, get a good night's sleep, and return after the weekend with a new resolve to master her tea leaves, to improve her tarot reading, and get back to the business of being a witch, and not allow herself to be distracted by her crush.

+···+···+···+···+···+

She was walking home from the Food Gryphon when he accosted her.

The black car was small and sporty, gleaming beneath the afternoon sunlight, the silver chrome grill nearly blinding her. They slid to the curb, idling beside her on the sidewalk, the window rolling down. Harper slowed but did not stop. She had been catcalled by creeps like this before.

"Get in, loser. We're going shopping."

It was Holt, leaning over the passenger seat with a grin. Harper scowled. *Literally being catcalled.*

"Uh, rude. I didn't tell you that I had to vacuum my furniture to get rid of the dander after you left the other day."

He dropped his head back and groaned. "I forgot, you're a fetus. Get in. We have errands to run. Starting with antidepressants, goddess knows you need them."

She scowled again but got into the car. To her surprise, he did not navigate back to the main road, taking what someone with a very poor sense of direction might have called a shortcut through several developments, snaking through Cambric Creek until they had reached Oldtowne.

"If you were just driving me home, you could've said so without being such a weirdo."

Holt looked askance from the corner of his eye, continuing past the street where her mother and sister lived, around the backside, past several of the large houses she admired on her evening walks until they arrived at the giant Second Empire edifice at the end of Magnolia.

"Are we going here?"

As soon as the words were out, Harper realized he was not pulling into the gated driveway of the stone mansion, but rather was backing into the driveway next door. The ornate Victorian she had admired, with the tower and gingerbread trim, huge sloping roofs, and fanciful exterior paintwork. She gulped, thinking of the huge shadow she'd seen in the third-floor windows. She trailed after him as Holt climbed the steps of the wide front porch, recently restored, she could tell. The front door had intricate millwork and a beautiful stained-glass transom, winking sidelights, and an elaborate brass knocker. *Brackenbridge*. The name tickled at the back of her mind, but she couldn't place how or why.

"Do you have arachnophobia?" Holt asked suddenly, glancing back at her with his eyebrows pulled together.

"I-I don't think so. Why?"

He let out the breath he'd evidently been holding, using the brass knocker to rap on the door before turning to her quickly. "Okay, look. I just need you to be cool, okay? I don't know what the fuck you kids say today, but no freakouts, all right? Your honor as a witch depends on it."

"Oh my word, what kind of place is this? Who are you taking me to?!"

Her question never received an answer, for just then, a frazzled-looking woman with a halo of frizzy curls and round glasses perched on the tip of her pert nose appeared hurrying down the hallway. She glanced out the sidelight, smiling when she saw Holt.

"Hello! Come in, come in. Gracious, did you bring her with you?! Well, that's fine. It'll make this easier. Come in, both of you. Holt, you know the way."

Harper followed him down the hallway, twisting through the house until they arrived at a large, spacious work kitchen. Harper did not know what her chief discipline would be if and when she returned to the Collegium. She had no affinity for her mother's crystals and had a feeling she was rather hopeless at divination, despite Azathé's optimism, but she knew the kitchen of the hedgewitch when she saw one, and this was perhaps the largest, most well-provisioned witch's kitchen she had ever seen with her own two eyes.

"You must be Harper," the woman said seriously, once she had come bustling in after them. "I'm so glad to meet you. Holt has told me all about you."

She threw a fast look at the familiar, who was too busy rummaging through the refrigerator to notice.

"I-I am. It's very nice to meet you, um . . ."

"Oh, how rude of me. Ladybug. Well, Ladybug is just a nickname. Elizabeth Amaranth Brackenbridge, but no one calls me that. I've been Ladybug since I was a little girl. My great-aunt tried calling me a Lilibet, but it never stuck. Ladybug has always been what I answer to."

She was babbling, but it was endearing. As she spoke, she lifted the lid off the cauldron that was bubbling over the work fire, her glasses steaming as she gave it a stir. Harper understood why her curls likely had a permanently frizzed appearance.

"Harper, do you have any allergies that you know of? Also, would you mind hopping on the scale over there next to the brick oven? Holt, if you eat those granola bars, I cannot promise what will happen to you. That is a choice between you and your maker, and it has nothing to do with me. Just putting that out there. And don't touch the coffee."

Harper grinned as Holt dropped the designer protein bar as if it were a hot coal. She stepped onto the scale, as instructed, wondering why she was doing so. "Um, no, I don't have any allergies. None that I'm aware of."

"Perfect. Okay, let me walk you through what we've cooked up. First of all, I have to disclose that I am not a medical doctor. I make no claims to the veracity of any of these herbal remedies, and if you have any concerns about abnormal heartbeat or lack of sleep, you should consult your physician. That being said, these recipes are hundreds of years old. Women like us have been treating their communities with these herbs since before there was even a word for doctor, so take that as you will."

"Um, sure, right."

"Perfect. So, we're going to start with the basics: zinc and magnesium, vitamin D and saffron, great mood boosters. The real magic starts to happen with the adaptogens. Now, with Rhodiola rosea, we use the roots. With St. John's wort, we use the flowers and leaves. I've made you a tisane using both. I hope you're a tea drinker."

At that, Harper laughed, still having no idea what this charming, awkward woman was babbling about. "You don't have to worry about that."

"Oh, good. That's good. That's a relief. Okay, so we're going to drink a tisane using the Rhodiola and St. John's wort.

You're going to drink this every morning, and we put the saffron, zinc, and vitamin D in a chewable. I just made it a fruity flavor, but if you don't care for it, we can change it. Then we have eleuthero and ashwagandha. Now, these are both plant extracts; one is a false ginseng, and the other is a winter cherry, but you're not going to be eating fruit. Just pop the capsules with your lunch. Then, at dinner, I want you to take your St. John's wort capsule. Don't worry, it's a safe dosage amount.

The Rhodiola and ashwagandha are both good for anxiety and stress. They increase your body's ability to adapt to stressful situations and environments. St. John's wort is for clinical depression, and I should tell you, it has proven just as effective as traditional antidepressants in several studies. All the headlines will tell you it wasn't any more effective than the placebo, but you usually have to read to the middle of the article to find out that the traditional drugs didn't perform better than the placebo either. So, we have mood regulators and stress adapters. These will help with your sleep and improve your overall energy. If you feel you are suffering from side effects from anything, don't hesitate to call me. We can always change up the recipe a bit. Each batch is formulated for the specific client. I'm also throwing in a bottle of my best-selling strawberry rose shampoo and conditioner. That doesn't have any health benefits, but it smells amazing."

By the time she was finished, Harper felt dizzy. The woman barely came up for air. The entire time she was explaining the different combinations of herbs and supplements, she worked at her cauldron, cutting and adding and stirring.

"Does-does that make sense? I'm sorry. I probably should have broken it up into little chunks. I'm not good at . . . Well, I'm not good at the actual client bit. But I have everything written out on cards for you, instructions on what to take and when and how much."

"Oh, you're fine. That was, like, ridiculously impressive? I only took core curriculum herbcraft, but I know it's really hard. You're giving big hospital doctor, whether you mean to or not."

The woman, Ladybug, smiled, her head dipping and her cheeks reddened.

"Um, how much do I owe you for all this?" Harper held her breath, waiting for the answer. Her weekly trips to the tearoom were beginning to cause a noticeable dent in her savings, and she was going to need to get off her ass and get a job sooner rather than later.

"Oh, there's no change, not yet. I want you to take everything and get into a routine with it, determine whether or not you feel like it's doing any good. Then we can set up a standing order."

"Are you sure? This is a lot, and you clearly put a lot of work into it already —" she cut off as Ladybug waved her protestation away.

"I'm sure. Like I said, Holt told me all about you. You're a sister in need of aid. That's all I need to know. And if you feel you want to continue on, we can set something up. Let's cross that bridge when we come to it."

Adjustments to the formulas needed to be made based on Harper's weight, and as Ladybug bent over her work-table, Harper pulled out one of the heavy-legged antique chairs. "Are you the coven's hedgewitch?"

"Oh! Oh, no. No, I don't belong to the coven. Not any-more."

She didn't say anything further, but Harper could sense it was not a happy story. She felt a rising tide of empa-thy within her for this incredibly kind woman. "Well, that makes two of us. I flunked out of school last term, and because I'm not actively enrolled, they won't let me attend coven meetings. They said I have to stay with the juniors until I am back in school, and I can't even begin to tell you how hard that is absolutely not going to happen. I'll take up snake handling first. I did my time in the Junior coven. It was horrible, and I'm never going back."

Ladybug laughed. "It really is the worst experience, right? I don't blame you. But I am sorry. I know what it feels like to be cast out, and it's not a kind thing to do to anyone, let alone a sister. Do you have plans to return to study?"

Harper mulled over how to answer. "I-I think so? Honestly, it changes from day to day. I have no idea what to focus on. Trying to work with divination right now, but I don't think I really have a natural talent for it."

"She's a shadowmancer."

Harper jerked at Holt's bored-sounding utterance. He was sitting on the countertop, stretching his arm against the cupboard, and she had a feeling that if he had been wearing his other skin, his leg would be over his head, licking himself.

"Oh! Well, that's very good. That's a rare skill, good for you."

Harper looked between the two of them, her mouth hanging open, not knowing how to answer. "I-I'm a what-?"

Holt rolled his eyes, hopping lightly to the floor. "You commune with the shadow folk. They do your bidding. Honestly, I'm not even sure how you manage to dress yourself in the morning."

"Holt!"

The woman sounded scandalized, but Harper just glared. *Fucking cats.*

"Rude."

From the work kitchen, they moved to a back hallway, dimly lit and thick with cobwebs. She couldn't imagine any part of this pleasant woman's home being full of dark corners, but there was something decidedly creepy about the thick webs against the walls.

"It's in pretty bad shape. There's a lot of water damage here. I'm not sure if a serious collector will be okay with that . . . I'll give you $300 for it."

Holt and Ladybug were standing in front of what appeared to be a carousel horse, a strange thing to keep in a hallway, but Harper decided she shouldn't judge. It was strange looking, even for a carnival ride. A grey-dappled horse with what looked like seaweed in its lacquered mane, its mouth opened in a snarl. She could never remember going on a carousel with horses that had sharp, jagged teeth, but different strokes for different folks.

"Are you out of your mind? Of course, there's water damage. It was pulled from the water! Add another zero to that, and maybe we'll talk."

He threw up his hands. "Be reasonable! I still have to sell it."

"You have to sell it, but that doesn't mean you get to rob me in the process. I don't think this is ethical anyway, I personally want nothing to do with it. I'm only the . . . the, um— "

"The fence," Holt grumbled.

"That's right. The fence. $1500 and not a penny less."

A thumping came from the ceiling above them, and Harper nearly dropped to the floor, worried the house was collapsing.

Ladybug sighed, shrugging blithely at Holt. "I mean $3000. Not a penny less."

They left a short while later, Holt making arrangements to pick up the creepy carousel horse later that week. The sky had already darkened, and the moon shone overhead as he drove Harper around the block.

"Do you want to go in the front or the back?"

"Um, the back, I guess. I have to explore the front in the afternoon when I can actually see where I'm going. Is it really the front door?"

"It is," he confirmed. "There is a flagstone path along the edge of the garden that leads right out on the sidewalk. It's easy to miss if you don't know what you're looking for."

"What are you going to do with that creepy horse?"

"Well, now I'm going to have to find a millionaire to buy it," he grumbled. "And it's not a horse. It's a kelpie. A very old kelpie. It's missing its trammel, so it was bound in those bones. I don't know how it got frozen like that, though. I have to do some research before we put it on the auction. I don't need to be sued because some hapless idiot gets eaten in their living room when it comes back to life in six months."

They arrived at the curb outside her mother's house, but Harper made no move to get out. Her head whipped around to the familiar, mouth dropping open. She pulled back his sleeve, ignoring his protest, when she held his hand up to the moonlight. Bone white, well-shaped, with long fingers. His tendons stood out in relief, sinuous and strong, capped by long, pointed black lacquered claws.

"It's you! From-from the auction!"

His eyes narrowed for the space of a heartbeat before his mouth split into a wide, sharp-toothed grin, and she understood why he was never featured on camera. He was attractive but unmistakably *other*, and humans would likely find his strange intensity and sharp teeth and claws off-putting.

"The Cat and Crow?" Holt nearly purred. "I'm one of the owners. You've watched our auctions?"

"I have! I watch it every week. Wait, who is that witch? Arabeth? Do you only work together?"

Holt rolled his eyes, and Harper wondered if he were in his other, four-legged form, he might hiss. *"Bethany,"* he enunciated derisively. "She's the one who abandoned her path. We no longer have a witch and familiar relationship. Purely co-owners. Although she's been talking about moving out west, so I might be buying her out. Why, do you want a job?"

"Yes!" she shouted, faltering a moment later. "Wait, I mean, I don't know. Yes, I do. But the shop is in Bridgeton, right?

That's a long train ride for a part-time job. I really love the shop, though. I mean, what I've seen online."

"Well, if you're serious, let me get back to you. I might have some remote work if you think you would be interested. It's nothing fun, I'll warn you now. Data entry, organizing spreadsheets, pricing research. Stuff like that. But you'll have to come out and visit us in person. All we feature on the auction are the curios. We keep a well-stocked supply of ritual aids and altar tools. Books on every discipline. A fine way for a solitary witch to continue her education."

Harper swallowed, nodding. *Who needs the Collegium?* She could work each day from the tea shop, she realized. Or, work for a few hours each morning here in her cottage, treating herself to lunch at Azathé to study her tea leaves. *The promise of a potential new coven and now maybe even a job. You ought to answer the door for strange men more often. Who knows, maybe he'll want you on full-time. You might be able to get a little apartment in Bridgeton, something close to the shop so that you can walk. You could come back to Cambric Creek every week on your day off to visit Morgan and read at the tea shop.*

"What did you think of her? She's a good egg, right?"

Harper shook herself back to attention. "Ladybug? Totally, she seems super sweet. Passes the vibe check. And she really knows her stuff. The coven is dumb to have let her go."

"She is an incredibly gifted witch," he agreed. "Not great at the social aspect, but that's window dressing. The courage of one's convictions is more important than their ability to engage in pointless small talk."

Harper nodded slowly, and he flashed her another grin.

"You may not have any talent for divination, Harper, but I do. Change is coming. Your skill will be valuable when it does."

"Do-do you really think I have a skill? I can't even make my sister do my bidding, and she's seven years younger than me."

Holt shrugged as she opened the car door, his white canines winking in the moonlight.

"I suppose you'll never find out unless you try."

Chapter 9

OOTD: Black and grey jumper dress with rabbit head buttons. Cap sleeve tee with ribbon trim. Grey striped knee socks and lug-sole loafers. Grey satin ribbon through braid and leaping hare ear cuff.

She got her chance at the end of the same month. It happened, as so many things did, when she stumbled upon the rest of the porn. Harper wasn't sure why she was surprised. After all, any literary collection of worth possessed at least one or two titles of erotica.

This, however, she thought, gazing at the shelves before her, was borderline excessive. *Excessive maybe, but entirely appreciated.* Making a mental note of where the books were located, she pulled a tarot deck from one of the shelves. She already had two tarot books on her table waiting for her and had only gotten up to look for an interesting deck to aid in her studies.

She wasn't sure what she had been expecting as she opened the deck, shuffling the cards with her eyes closed. She wasn't sure what she had been expecting, but the images that met her eyes when they opened were not it. *But again, appreciated.* The staid, familiar illustration style was the same as the Rider Waite deck, but those characters had never seemed this scandalous before.

The Three of Cups — an enthusiastic threesome. The Empress — a regal figure on her throne, her pomegranate-bedecked robe thrown open and her legs spread wide as several attendants of various gender and species licked her. The One of Wands – a woman on her knees, fellating a single man. The Six of Wands – the same woman, still on her knees, sinking down onto a veined dildo, holding another to her lips, with the remaining four scattered around her. Harper nearly swooned.

Depression was fickle and tricksy, and when it held her in its grip, all she wanted to do was sleep until she practically forgot her own name. *But.* The potions and tinctures and teas from the awkward witch's kitchen were working. She rose each day with more energy, a little more enthusiastic to be out of bed at all, and most importantly, she had begun to see the difference between her depression and her grief.

Grief was an ocean inside her, a bruise on her heart, and as Holt had told her, to poke it ached. She never knew where the poke might come from — the same woodsmoke smell from her neighbor's yard that comforted her as she slept had made her nearly choke on her tears as she sat cross-legged on the chair beside her alleged front door one evening, remembering the times she had assisted her father in the forge. *Someday these memories will make you smil*e.

An oldies song they had always sung together at the top of their lungs whenever it came on in the car had forced her into the grocery store's parking lot, basket abandoned on the floor of the frozen aisle, her shoulders heaving. *You're going to sing this same song with your kid or with Morgan's kids someday, and you can tell them that you used to sing it with their grandfather.* The bruise ached as bruises were wont to do, but grief, she reminded herself, was a gift, and her heart was a resilient thing.

"You okay?"

The girl had been leaning on the side of an older model car that had seen better days a decade earlier in the Food Gryphon parking lot, barely able to hold the butt of the cigarette she was smoking down to her fingertips. She looked to be Harper's age, perhaps a few years older. She wore a fishnet top beneath a black tank, a frayed smoke-colored denim skirt, and thick soled combat boots. Her eyes were heavily lined in black; her hair dyed the same, with the exception of her thick, candy apple red bangs. The overall effect was haphazard, but Harper appreciated the efforts of a fellow goth, no matter how on point.

She nodded after a moment, sucking in a shuddering breath. "Yeah. Thanks. Real life got a little too real there for a second." The girl nodded as if she understood, and perhaps, Harper considered, she did. "I love your bag. Did you get it around here somewhere?" The black tote was embroidered with the phases of the moon in luminous silver, and beneath it was a spray of soft green Luna moths.

"I made it." The girl fished in the bag with her free hand, coming up with a card that she passed to Harper a moment later. *The Black Veil ~ Occultist Artistry.* She looked up in surprise.

"Are you from the coven?"

One last pull from the cigarette, the butt deposited in the empty water bottle on her dashboard. "Nope. Should I be?"

"Yeah," she chuckled, eyeing the glyphs on the card. "Probably. Well, hold that thought. I'm not from the coven, they kicked me out. But I guess a new one is starting soon? I can give you a call when it does."

The girl smiled, and looked at least a decade younger when she did. "Nice. I'll definitely check it out, especially if it's the misfits club. For a weird town, there aren't nearly enough weirdos around."

"Agreed. I'm Harper, by the way."

"Lex. I guess I need to head in there. Wish me luck, there's usually a panic attack waiting somewhere around the cereal aisle."

"Good luck. Don't let real life get too real."

"Yeah, you too," the girl laughed as she pushed off the car, making for the automatic doors.

Grief was a bruise on her heart, but her heart was still capable of doing other things.

Depression, on the other hand . . . depression lied. Depression was that little lizard voice at the back of her consciousness that was always quick to cut her down and remind her of her shortcomings. Depression was losing half a week to her bed, believing the hateful, poisonous things Ilea said, that she wasn't a good enough witch, a good enough sister, a good enough daughter.

Depression was a blanket that cocooned her, but when the melancholy passed, it left her body writhing like an exposed nerve, and she was desperate to be fucked. Fucked and licked and fucked again, held down and used, over and over until she was exhausted and sated and finally felt as though she was not going to go mad from her inability to sit still.

Her body was like a live wire as she stared in shock at the cards that day in the tearoom, and she was unable to sit still without unconsciously canting her hips, seeking the friction she desperately needed. Harper stared down at the blissed-out look on the illustrated woman's face, the lips of her sex parting for the head of her toy, and she wondered if she ought to go home and do the exact same thing, putting distance between herself and the sinuous shadows.

"How is our divination study going today?"

She jumped, blood draining from her face as she squirmed in her seat. They never made any sound on their approach, but normally Harper was able to discern a brief ripple of movement through the shadows that denoted their approach. Not today, clearly. Not when she was so distracted.

"It's, um, it's" — she swallowed hard, willing herself to control — "going well?"

Beside her, Azathé huffed. "I see you have found one of the erotic decks."

"I did. It's quite . . . instructional."

They harrumphed again, and she squirmed "What are you reading today?"

"I'm not really reading anything," Harper shrugged. "I tried picking something at home, but nothing looked good. And there are too many choices here. I was just going to study the cards. I pulled a few books with new spreads that I haven't tried yet, but I don't know how much work I'm going to get done. I guess I'm a bit distracted today."

The shadows rustled beside her, and for the briefest moment, Harper was certain they were about to pull into a physical form.

"Too many choices seem preferable to too few, does it not? A wide selection of choices is what light walkers prefer, I thought? Why, just look at our menu, we have more than a hundred different looseleaf options that you might pick from —"

"Yeah, and it's about eighty-five too many on some days. At least for me. You're right, a lot of people love having a big selection to pick from, no matter what it is — books, tea, brands of crackers, the exact same flavor of soda from eight different brands. I'm not one of them, though. Too many choices are overwhelming."

They were flummoxed. The little noises of offense coming from the corner were like bursts of electricity across her skin, crinkled paper and a staticky radio. "But — but that doesn't make any —"

"It doesn't need to make sense to you. That's just how I am. Some people like choices. I like being told what to do. Pin me down and take all my choices from me, that sounds like a perfect afternoon."

Her cheeks heated as the words came out, not that they weren't true. She was still staring in envy at the Six of Wands, the woman lowering herself on the fat, veined cock. Harper thought she seemed a bit smug, and she understood why.

"Have you already finished the Volantines?"

She swallowed, face heating. "I did. I have some follow-up questions on that one, but not today. I need to organize my thoughts a bit better. As I said, I'm feeling a bit distracted this afternoon."

"Then I suppose you will simply have to pull for a reading. Otherwise, how are we to know what you're drinking today? In the meantime, go to the mouth of the solarium. Just inside to your left, on the first shelf. There is a book of poetry I think you might enjoy."

She sucked in the deep breath as soon as they left the table, crossing the room to attend to the other two patrons in the shop at that moment. They had been there for a bit, already had their tea, and she was certain it wouldn't be long before they left, and she had the shop and its shadowy proprietor all to herself.

She did not need to be told what to do upon their return, nor did she need to be told about the return itself. She felt the exact moment when their energy slid into the shadow of her table, could discern the thickness in the corner, the faintest change in color. Perhaps Holt was right. She was actually good at something.

Harper knew the drill. She was not new to any of this, and she did not need to read the instructional placard. *Shuffle the deck. Cut from the center. Choose three cards, one at a time, and place them in the template. Do not touch the rest of the cards once they have been returned to the basket.* She shuffled the deck. She cut from the center. When the first card she drew was the devil, Harper decided she was potentially going to die of bang-xiety.

The card depicted the typical couple, loosely shackled at Baphomet's feet, but instead of the typical trappings of worldly possessions, they were on their knees, fucking like animals as the horned devil looked on. She shifted, scarcely able to hold still, wanting nothing more than to drop to her knees and present herself like a bitch in heat.

"Temptation at its most carnal. Hedonistic pleasure, heedless of the consequences."

The priestess had been taken in such a way by her demon lover, and it was clear to Harper by the midway point of the book that her lover was absolutely what the summoned entity was. Her face had been pressed into the dust of the temple floor, her ass pulled high in the air as the demon squatted on his haunches behind her, hips thrusting with the force that nearly knocked the priestess over. Harper wondered for the millionth time since finishing the book if Azathé could do the same.

"Hedonistic pleasure, but debauchery does not come free of cost. Desire and lust can lead to obsession without temperance."

The second card was the Eight of Swords. The swords were normally a suit of despair, but not in this deck. While the suit of Wands was phallic in nature, the suit of Swords reveled in the pleasure of pain. The Eight card featured a blindfolded and bound woman, normally the symbol of subjugation and abuse, but the woman on this card was having an altogether different experience. She was still bound and blindfolded, but instead of being huddled on a bed in a dark room or bound to a pike, as she was often depicted in other decks, this woman was spread eagle, bound to a St. Andrew's cross. Her mouth was open in an expression of delight, red marks on her skin from the eight swords around her, her sex on display.

Harper squirmed. She had never been a fan of S&M and was not particularly interested in discovering the limits of her pain threshold now, but she did want to be dominated. She wanted to be as helpless as the bound woman, held down as she was fucked, unable to free herself, used for someone else's pleasure.

She had always thought it was one of those kinks that was too shameful to be shared aloud, verging too closely with nonconsensual acts, and she had woken in too many beds with no recollection of how she got there or of ever having said yes to court non-consent without a clear mind. Being freed from the burden of choice, however, was an altogether different thing. She would only give the power to someone she trusted, and there was no one she trusted more than the shadow in the corner beside her.

"An absence of control over one's circumstances. Perhaps sexual slavery or some other heinous act."

"No." Her eyes popped open, the sound of her own voice surprised her, but she could not allow the fantasy playing out in her head to be tainted. "That's not what it means. It's willingly giving up control. Allowing yourself to be used for someone else's pleasure and finding your own pleasure in the act of being dominated. It's the freedom of not having to choose."

Another burst of that crinkled harrumph beside her. "Again, with the choices? In my experience, human nature values free will above all."

"It's not giving up your free will," Harper interrupted. "It's-it's being freed of having to make decisions. Trusting someone enough to give them your choices and knowing they will take care of you."

"And this is why you ordered the green wellness tea for more than a month?" they demanded, making her laugh.

"That's exactly why. And I trusted you to make the decision for me. I still do. And I know that you'll take care of me. I have very simple needs."

"And those are?"

Harper shrugged, grinning, her lips pressed together. *You'll never know unless you try.* "Good books. Hot tea. Someone to call me a good girl as they hold me down and fuck me into next month. Maybe one of those little fruit tarts. Hot soup. A pumpkin on my doorstep. Very simple needs."

Azathé was quiet as she pulled her third and final card, and she wondered if she had shocked them into silence, or if they were contemplating her words.

Her last card was Temperance, not what she had been expecting. Unlike some of the other cards' overt displays of carnality, the Temperance card showed a pair of lovers in silhouette, stretched out on a bed. They were clearly engaged in intercourse, but their fingers were threaded, their limbs intertwined, in harmony together.

"The serenity of this card compared to the others shows the importance of balance." Their voice was a velvet whisper. Harper shivered as it tickled up her spine, settling around her like a plush blanket. " A perfect mix of action and passivity, excitement and relaxation. Submission and domination, both freely given, balance in all things, my sweet one."

"That's the dream," Harper murmured. "Have you ever heard of something called a shadowmancer?"

A crackle of static, shadows shifting and pooling, hooking around her ankle in a way that made her jump it simultaneously felt familiar and secure.

"A cat I know told me that's what I am. They said it's because I commune with the shadows. I can make you do my bidding. Is that true? Are you going to do my bidding if I order it?"

"You only need to ask it of me, and I will do it for you, little one. An order is not necessary. And I've already told you, your ability is extremely rare."

Harper felt her heart do something in her chest, the reverberation like timpani throughout her body, vibrating in her jaw, rattling her teeth, making her vision wobble. The shadow hooked around her ankle felt as if it belonged there. "Have you followed me home before?"

A long pause. "Yes," they admitted at last, the word coming out as a hiss. "I was concerned."

"Why? What were you concerned over?"

"You were in such despair, little one, when you first began coming here. I was concerned you were considering doing yourself an injury."

Her eyes filled with tears, recalling that endless, glasslike sea. "I think I was."

"What caused you to change your mind, I wonder?"

"The shadows started talking to me," she murmured, tears leaving salty tracks down her cheeks. "And I started answering back."

She felt the darkness crowd around her, enveloping her for a moment, and the waking world disappeared. A curl at her ear and a chill at her cheek, like a kiss from a ghost. "Good girl."

+ · · · + · · · + · · · + · · · + · · · +

Her nerves were jangling as she walked home that night. She wandered around downtown until the very last trolley that would take her back to Oldetowne pulled away from the gazebo, a curious weight hooked around her ankle. It stayed there as she stalked through the streets of her twilight-lit neighborhood, until the stars began to wink overhead, and it was too dark for the shadows to gather.

She took the long way around, finding the little pathway Holt had told her about, entering her home through the front door for the first time. It looked like a proper witch's house. *It should. Because you are a proper witch.*

Undressing while knowing she had an audience was a foreign sensation. She had never been into exhibitionism, wouldn't know how to be alluring if someone paid her to do so, and was pretty sure she would look like an awkward, newly plucked chicken if she attempted to be seductive, whatever that entailed.

Instead, Harper simply took her time. After all, that was the killer, right? She felt ready to combust from bang-xiety, and tightening the winch by slowing the pace would only increase the tension, sweetening the payoff in the end.

She carefully slid the lacquered rabbit ear buttons through their holes, sliding the jumper dress down her body. Her shoes had already been replaced in their box on her shoe shelf in the closet, her ear cuff carefully laid onto the velvet cushion of her jewelry box, her hair ribbon placed in its bowl.

She had learned very early in her scholastic career as a witch that goth girls like herself were a dime a dozen. What set her apart, Harper thought with pride, was her attention to detail, her careful matching of colors, her eclectic mix of accessories, and the care she took with her shoes and handbags. That was always when she knew her depression had reached its nadir — when she no longer cared about taking care of her clothes, when she kicked off her shoes at the door and left them laying in a haphazard heap rather than carefully unlacing them, pulling them off with her hands instead of breaking down the heels, replacing them in their boxes so that they stayed clean and scuff free. Some people needed pets. She needed patent leather pumps and delicate lace dusters.

Once her dress was hung up, Harper lifted her foot to the side of her bed, slowly rolling her knee socks down her legs, exposing her milky white "I haven't seen the sun since toddlerhood" skin an inch at a time. Her bra was next, deftly unhooking it through her shirt, slipping her arms free of the straps and pulling the whole thing from the bottom of her shirt, following her socks into the hamper. *Now or never. You'll never know unless you try.* Gripping the bottom hem of her shirt, she pulled the fabric up her body at a snail's pace, arching her back as she did so to give her breasts the best silhouette possible. Her panties were the last to go, and then she was bare to the room, bare to the world, vulnerable and exposed to shadows.

If she had thought they would pounce the instant she began undressing, she would have been wrong. *Of course not. They want to make sure you want this first.*

Harper climbed to the center of her bed, staring up at the ceiling. Azathé had made no move to come out of the shadows, and she wondered briefly if she had imagined the weight sitting around her ankle as she walked home. *No.* She knew that she hadn't. The invisible shackle had slithered free, disappearing into the dark corners of the room as soon as the door had swung shut behind her, and she could feel the crackle of their energy still.

Pretend you're alone. What would you be doing if you were home alone right now? She closed her eyes and envisioned that tarot deck again. The Six of Pentacles – self-care and luxury. A figure stretched out on their bed, just as she was, legs splayed, pleasuring themselves with their hand. The Eight of Swords – blindfolded and restrained, hands tied down and legs open, at the mercy of whoever might have her.

Harper opened her legs, placing her feet at opposite sides of the mattress, as if she were tied to the bed posts. With one hand, she stroked down her body, a slow fingertip over her neck, down the valley between her breasts, moving over each creamy mound to circle her nipples. She kept her eyes closed and her other hand raised over her head, as if it, too, were restrained. *Show them what you want. Show them what you want them to do.*

Down her stomach, across the dark triangular thatch neatly trimmed hair, and then — heat, stroking through her silky hot folds, coating fingers in her slickness. She slid two fingers into herself, pumping her wrist once, twice, her hips raising from the bed on the third, a small cry breaking from her throat. She dragged the moisture upward, using her fingertips to rub circles over clit until she was hardly able to hold still, the effort of keeping her feet to the bed hard without an actual restraint. When she moaned again, the shadows finally shifted.

Harper's eyes popped open, sensing the movement, watching as a black mass swirled at the foot of her bed coalescing before her. Dense and black with a tar-like malleability, shifting as she watched. Watched and waited. One arm, then two, then six, the stretch of what may have been wings, the writhe of what were surely tentacles, the blink of over a dozen eyes. It was like nothing she could have imagined, but somehow, everything she'd been dreaming of. When they finally settled on a form, Azathé had a vaguely humanoid outline, although the stretch of many arms still blurred her eyes with their speed.

They advanced on the bed slowly, shadows unspooling like ribbons. Harper's breath caught when one wrapped around her ankle, a tentacle-like appendage of inhuman strength, holding her down. When a second tentacle trapped the other foot, her core clenched in exhilaration and readiness. Yes. This was what she wanted. The absence of control, freedom of having to use her broken brain to make any decisions, placing her pleasure and her safety in the hands of someone she trusted with her life. They had already proven themselves to be an excellent steward of her heartbeat, even without her knowing.

"Is this what you want, my sweet one? Is this the submission you are craving?"

Her breath was already coming out in hitching little pants and they hadn't even done anything yet. "Y-yes. I want you to hold me down."

Another one of those unspooling tentacles closed around her wrists, holding them over her head, pinned to the pillows.

"Then what?"

"Whatever you want to do to me. Use me for your pleasure. Make me scream."

She wasn't sure what they were going to do, but bracing themselves around her, missionary style, was not what she expected. Arms around her like cages, long fingers threading with her own, where they were pinioned above her head. Another set of hands, tipped in long claws with the consistency of smoke, cupped her breasts, rolling her hardened nipples until she gasped. At her neck, another snaking tentacle from their mouth, icy cold, licking at her neck.

"You're going to work on your tasseomancy when we're done." Their voice was stern, the order non-negotiable, and she nodded like a bobble-headed doll, quickly agreeing. A cool pressure against her cheek, the closest they could come to kissing her. "Good girl."

Harper assumed they would model their shape after one of the tarot cards, perhaps the thick cock gripped on the Ace of Pentacles – sprouted from the base of the card, gripped in a woman's hand, veined with a fat mushroom head. Harper prepared herself.

She was not expecting a second tongue. Her head dropped back, mouth open as the tongue delved into her folds, licking against her clit like a cat with a bowl of cream. It was also icy cold, but as it fastened around her pussy like a seal, she felt heat bubbling within her. Harper thought of the priestess, writhing on her stone plinth as her demon lover's forked tongue flicked against her clit, and felt as if she were there in that torch-lit temple, her cunt feasted on by an inhuman mouth. Azathé's tongue worked against her, one tongue at her clit, the other at her throat, her arms and legs pinned down by their steel like tentacles, and she moaned.

It was then that it filled her. Another tentacle, she realized, one as thick as a cock, pushing into her slowly, stretching her walls against its intrusion, the flickering pressure against her clit never slowing. The tentacle inside her began to move, wriggling as it fucked her, catching at her G spot as if the tentacle itself had sprouted a miniature tongue, and Harper thought perhaps it had. It assumed a frantic pace, moving against her G spot and her clit in tandem, the thickness of the appendage making her wheeze. Their hands squeezed her breasts, icy cold breath at her neck, teeth as insubstantial as the wind at her jaw. If Ilea had a mind to go snooping around outside her window that night, they would hear the unmistakable wet squelch of a deep fucking, and it would serve them right.

Harper thought of that night in the library, how quickly she had fallen apart against Kel's mouth, the newness of the experience overwhelming her and how embarrassed she was after. That night, compared to the way she was feeling at the present, had been a marathon sex session, and she ought to have won a gold medal for her longevity and stamina. The sensation of being held down and fucked would have been enough to make her come. Adding the tongue at her clit and whatever the *fuck* was licking her from the inside? Harper felt as if her bones were going to melt. It was overwhelming, and she needed to come before she died.

She would have time to be embarrassed later, as her eyes rolled back, another tentacle no bigger than her pinky finger pushing against the cleft of her ass, wriggling into her and making her buck against her restraints.

Her muscles clenched, pussy convulsing, and the world went white. Her back arched against her mattress, shaking as if she had been electrocuted, the tentacles inside her still moving, still fucking, still licking, not backing off until she practically sobbed, sagging boneless against the sheets.

All at once, everything receded. Her head lolled and her arms, all pins and needles from having been held in place, were rubbed gently as the pooled blood spread and feeling came back. Harper found herself swaddled in her comforter, tucked against her pillows like an infant, hand in her hair, hand at her back, hand gently stroking her cheek, and then the shadows shifted again. Azathé was across the room, putting the tea kettle on the stove.

"Sit up slowly." Another command, albeit softer, a gentle whisper that curled around her. She was trembling when they handed her the cup. "Are you all right, sweet one?"

Harper nodded. The absence of control, given to someone who would care for it. She had chosen well.

"And is that what you wanted?"

"That's exactly what I wanted." She leaned against them, allowing herself to be wrapped in several sets of arms, a ribbon like shadow hooking around her ankle, a comfortable, familiar weight. "Was — was that okay? I mean, for you?" They had not experienced any sort of climax, and Harper wondered if they were even able to do so. "Do you even feel any pleasure from sex?"

"Did *you* experience pleasure, little witch?"

"Yes," she laughed without hesitation. "Absolutely, over-whelmingly yes. That was amazing. But . . . but I don't want to do something if you don't enjoy —"

"If I am here to watch you experience pleasure, does not some of the pleasure become mine, having experienced it through you?"

Harper didn't have an answer. It must have been lonely, watching the world from afar. Being a part of it, but removed at the same time, invisible and unnoticed.

"If Temperance means balance in all things, don't you think you should split your time equally between our world and the shadows?"

The sound of their scoff was like leaves shaking on their branches. "I already spend more time in the topside world than most of my brethren."

"Yeah, well, if little Johnny Shadowbutt decides to jump off a bridge, are you going to do it too?"

"That is nonsensical."

"No, it makes perfect sense! Balance in all things. You are a silent observer of everyone in town. It's really not fair. People wouldn't reveal their confidences over their lunch if they knew someone was standing over their shoulder listening. I think you should be a part of this world too, part of *my* world, and actually *be* a part of it. I can't be the only one you talk to. Right now, you are Temperance reversed. All or nothing. I'm not saying you need to start wearing the three-piece suit and calling yourself Ezekiel. You are of the shadow realm, and that is where you're comfortable, I get it. But if two decades in the junior coven taught me nothing else, it's you have to be comfortable with being uncomfortable. Balance. Temperance."

"I think you should find balance in drinking your tea."

"You're the one who said the ability to read the cards is of vital importance!" Harper shot back, scowling over the rim of her cup.

"Perhaps I did," they allowed, "but your tea is getting cold, and the study of no subject is worth that."

"But I can't be the only—" She cut off on a gasp, her wrists gripped not ungently, her teacup held by an arm coming out of the center of what was shaped like their chest.

"*You*, my little witch," they said in a serpentine curl, "are *always* enough."

Chapter 10

O OTD: Pleated-front high-waist gabardine shorts with suspenders. Swiss dot chiffon crop top with pussycat bow. Knee-length black cardigan with white pumpkin design, because this is MY season. Sheer thigh-highs with pumpkin trim. Stacked heel ankle boots. BFE — Big Fall Energy.

The bell over the doorway was not a bell at all. A melodic gong sounded somewhere from deep within the shop, alerting one of the sisters to her presence. Harper sucked in a slow breath, relishing the cool, green scent of the place. Potting soil and green leaves, herbaceous and refreshing.

"Good afternoon! What brings you in today?"

The smiling beetlewoman before her didn't possess a single shred of recognition in her eyes, and Harper reminded herself that there were two of them. *This probably isn't the sister you talked to the last time you were here. Or maybe it is, and she doesn't remember you. That's not some moral failing on your part. It doesn't mean you are unmemorable or worthless. It means she works in retail and talks to dozens of customers a week and can't be expected to remember every single one of them.*

"Hi. Um, I think I want to get a succulent? In one of those little stone dishes?"

The beetlewoman raised her hand to direct Harper toward the aisle of spiky little plants, when the stockroom door swung open, two more identical women stepping out.

"Ah, our literature lover! Change your mind about having a fellow introvert as a roommate?"

She grinned hugely, heat moving up her neck. *See? You're completely memorable.*

"I did, actually. I think I want some of those little rosettes, as long as they don't need any sort of extra –"

"Nope. They want to sit in the corner by the window and meditate on the weather. A perfect choice."

Harper trailed after the woman once the dish of succulents was acquired from the shelf, following her back to the register. As the pretty beetlewoman scanned a barcode at the bottom of the dish, one of her sisters began prepping the packaging. They were dressed identically, all in black, and Harper took note of their silk-blend cardigans, fitted pencil skirts, and satin blouses — all perfectly coordinated, cardigan matching the skirt without a hint of poor color coordination. *These are your people.*

"I didn't realize there were three of you," she laughed awkwardly.

"Oh, yes! The Viol," the beetle woman gestured to the sisters still standing in the aisle, "The violet," to herself, "And the vine," to the sister stuffing a small square box with tissue paper. "This is the customer I mentioned earlier this summer, who knows our poem."

Harper smiled. *Your moment to shine and show the world what a gothic little nerd you really are.* "Lo, death has reared himself a throne, in a strange city lying alone."

She was unprepared for the sisters to take up the verse, speaking in tandem, as if in a chant:

"Far down, within the dim West,"

"Where the good —"

"And the bad —"

"And the worst —"

"And the best —"

"Have gone to their eternal rest."

Harper let out a low sound of wonder. "Wow. And I thought *I* was an edge lord."

The three sisters laughed, and the strange moment was broken.

"What made you choose that poem specifically? It doesn't exactly bring to mind plants and flowers." She pulled out her credit card as the two sisters behind the register shrugged in unison.

"I'm not sure, really. Just always resonated with us. You know, we grew up here. I always used to think that poem was specifically about Cambric Creek."

"With Jack in his shining golden tower, looking down on the town," the second sister laughed.

"But now," the first sister went on, ignoring the second, "I think of it more as a warning of what can happen to a place if we're corrupted by greed and selfishness and stop caring for each other. We've heard whispers of quite a bit of that going around lately. But Poe was part gnomish, so who can even guess."

"I think it's a reflection on human nature," Harper murmured, "'No swellings tell that winds may be, Upon some far-off happier sea.'" She thought of that still, glass-like sea swaying within her. She could let it drown her, and sink . . . or she could swim, and pull herself from the waters. She glanced up, cheeks heating. "I-I don't mean *human* nature, specifically, but like —"

"I know what you mean," the first sister assured her with a small smile. "There are some things that transcend species, after all. Well, I am very glad that you came back. Remember — this is an introvert. She does not want to go for drinks three times a week, go to the beach, sit out in the sun, or have a party with her other friends. She wants to sit by the window and read and be left alone."

"Sounds like the dream," Harper laughed. "That's goals. Thank you. If she makes it to her third month birthday with no setbacks, maybe I'll get her a friend to sit and ignore."

"That's the way to do it," the sister standing in the aisle laughed. "The three of us will be sitting in the same room all night long on our phones, texting each other, not saying a word."

A sound of rippling, identical laughter followed her out the door.

"I know just where I'm going to put you," she murmured, thinking of the little pedestal table she'd rescued from someone's curb the night before trash pickup. "But first, we have a stop to make."

+ · · · + · · + · + · · · + · · · + · · · +

"Balance in all things" was a challenge they had taken to heart.

After that night in her cottage, they settled into a new routine. She would time her visits to Azathé later in the day, which just a few months earlier would have meant an excuse to stay in bed until the middle of the afternoon. Now, though, she had to get up and make her tea. Ladybug had been specific in her instructions, noting the set intervals in which she was meant to take the herbal concoctions, and Harper wasn't about to impede her own progress by slipping into old habits.

Besides, she found that she *liked* being up and productive. Her recent discoveries at home took up most of her morning and early afternoon, and by the time the two p.m. chimes reverberated from the restored grandfather clock that now stood in the basement, she would be eager to set off for the tearoom. She would arrive shortly before closing, settling in a quiet corner with a tarot deck and her tea, waiting for them to join her.

Once the door was locked after the final patron and the velvet curtains pulled across the front windows, they would melt from the shadows, assuming a physical form to sit beside her.

"Isn't this nice?" she asked with a sigh, eyes fluttering closed.

The tea they had selected for her that day was a blended green. Long, tightly rolled leaves, dotted with great hunks of pungent red fruit, the aroma of the dried strawberries heady in her nose.

She understood their reasoning for remaining shadow-bound during the shop's hours of operation — the invisible hands that pushed the tea cart, the feline hostess, the air of mystery that surrounded the scrolls and tarot cards and spirit boards — that was why people came back. She herself admitted if they had been a typical restaurant with average servers, she might have only ventured in that one afternoon.

She understood the reason . . .But after closing, *she* was in charge.

"A powerful familiar told me I'm a shadowmancer and you have to do my bidding. My bidding is for you to get physical, so step to it."

They would grumble and grouse in their way, a sibilant susurration, but the shadows would swirl and coalesce, settling into the shape they seemed most comfortable with — humanoid, tall and slender, with two sets of arms and half a dozen trailing tentacles. She thought it was adorable that they had no idea what constituted *normal*, but she wasn't going to do anything to change the shape they had chosen. *It is uniquely theirs, and it's perfect.*

"There's jam to have with your scone," they whispered, the rattle of the windows on a windy, stormy night, and she noticed the little pot of strawberry jam they'd placed on the table for the first time, sitting next to the clotted cream, the scone resting on a lace doily.

Drawing three cards from the shuffled deck before her, taking a bite of her jam and cream-slathered scone, Harper placed them in a line. The Star, the Chariot reversed, and the Hanged Man.

"An auspicious draw, my sweet one."

"It is, isn't it," Harper mused, taking another bite of her scone. "The Star."

"A foot on the earth," Azathé gestured, "a foot in the water. Balance in all things. The Star is one of the most optimistic cards in the deck. Look at the goodness surrounding her. It is easy to overlook the bounty in one's life, but consider — the Star follows the Lightning-Struck Tower. Devastation and trauma. There will always be hard times to navigate in this life —"

"But things will always get better if you let them." She nodded. Her father used to tell her the same thing. "This one makes me nervous, though."

"The Chariot. Two opposing forces that we must control. If you allow one to win over, you'll never move forward. Reversed, it tells us —"

"I swear to the mother, if you tell me balance in all things one more time," Harper laughed. "Why do I get the feeling that the great myth of tarot is the cards all mean the same godsdamn thing?"

Their laughter was a pleasant buzz against her skin, and for a moment, they lost their form, nothing more than a swirling black shape before her, reforming a heartbeat later. A curling tendril of smoke wrapped around her ankle.

"You are not wrong, little witch. Balance is, I'm afraid, the answer to most of life's ills. Sweet with the sour and laughter to temper your pain. The Hanged Man . . . A sacrifice needed? Perhaps you must set aside your own desires in order to achieve something more important?"

"No," Harper murmured, shaking her head. "Here, it means taking my time. Letting a new relationship progress as slowly as it requires to feel comfortable." She glanced up, watching their form waver across the table. "I know I said this is what I want," she gestured to their corporeal presence at the table, "but-but if it makes you uncomfortable, or if it's too much right now —"

"You know, little witch, someone very wise recently taught me that the *absence* of choice is sometimes a gift we bestow on those who mean the most to us. Allowing them to make the choice for us, and trusting them to take care of us. It seems to me that having that trust in another must be the deepest measure of love and affection."

Her heart thrummed in her chest as if it had sprouted wings like a beautiful black butterfly. "It is. I would never give my choices to someone I didn't trust entirely, and I can only trust someone if I love them."

"Quite right," they hummed.

She walked home that evening carrying the bag containing her little dish of spiky green rosettes, with a comfortable, familiar weight around her ankle.

"Is there really such a thing as a shadowmancer?" she asked, once she was stretched in her bed, shadows pressed to her back. Harper was comfortable being the little spoon and did not crane her head over her shoulder to see the form they had taken. It did not matter. "He's super inspiring, but I won't pretend that Holt doesn't have a dash of sus. I may have been born at night, but I wasn't born last night. Cats can't be trusted, so I don't know if he was just yanking my chain."

Cold fingertips walked down her spine, making her shiver. She wondered if it was cold in the shadow realm, and if they found the topside world intolerably warm.

"There is certainly such a thing, my sweet one. Regrettably, for your career aspirations, I don't know that I would consider you to be one, although, you possess the predisposition, should you choose to seek it."

"What the actual fuck is that even supposed to mean?!"

They chuckled, low dark, plush velvet pressing to her back. "I have already told you, little witch. Most people cannot see the things that dwell in the shadows. Your ability to do so is quite rare, particularly as it is not a skill it seems you have studied. The majority of topsiders who can see my brethren can only do so once we have made ourselves known, taking form, as I have done for you."

She shrugged. "I already told you; most people can't match blacks. They go out of the house thinking they look chic and put together, but they actually look like a patchwork clown."

"Yes, well, your fashion predilections aside, I assure you, your ability is not common. If one of the shadowfolk entered your home, you might not notice them immediately, but you would eventually. Movement from the corner of your eye that most would not notice, a darkening of corners —"

"It's not only that," she interrupted. "You have a different energy. It's like . . . an electric charge. Static against my skin, like if you rub a balloon against your arm. It makes your hair stand out, yes, but you also feel that crackle against you. But yes, I can also see the difference in color of an empty shadow and one that you're in."

They shifted behind her, seeming slightly discomfited by her disclosure.

"I have never heard it described in such a way. As I said, little witch, you have a rare talent. A dangerous one, in the wrong hands."

Harper twisted again. "What does *that* mean?"

Azathé shrugged, a shifting of the shadows around her, rising and falling gently, like a pile of soot. "It means precisely what your feline friend indicated. There have been those in existence who are able to bind the shadows to their will. It is advanced witchcraft, but one cannot do so if they don't naturally possess the skill to see the shadows in the first place."

Harper was quiet, chewing over their words and her lip in the process. She felt an uncomfortable twist within her, the sense that she had unfairly coerced them rising in her throat like bile.

"Is-is that why so many of you stay hidden?"

"That is part of it, yes," they admitted.

She swallowed hard, feeling wretchedly guilty over her insistence that they assume a physical form to exist in the world beside her. *What if something happens to them because of you?*

"I can tell what's going through your head, sweetling, and I assure you, my reticence has nothing to do with a fear of being lassoed by some dark wizard, as if I were no more than a sheep. My kind are watchers. That is what we do. We watch the world around us, much in the same manner as the trees do. Don't ever be fooled into thinking a tree does not have its own consciousness, little one. The trees stand tall in the world and watch over it silently, and we watch silently from the darkness. We stay hidden for much the same reason that the fair folk remain on the other side of the veil. It is hard to know you, for to know you is to love you, and parting is sorrowful, no matter your species."

Another twist within, the sea rocking, a poke to her bruise.

"It hardly seems fair," she murmured, pressing herself into the shadow at her back. Harper could feel their wavering solidity, slipping through them one moment, being buffeted against them in the next. "It doesn't make any sense for us all to have such different lifespans. Hours and days and weeks mean nothing to you immortals, and those of us who have to count every second have so few of them."

"Immortality doesn't exist, dear one. All things end. Even me. My sort were not born into existence, we simply *exist*. Once there was a great void of darkness, and on to it the light shone, from which sprung all life. Shadows cannot exist without light. The construct of immortality is predicated upon a short span of time, but I assure you, all things have their natural ending. The shadow folk, the fair folk, even the sea. Someday there will be a darkness that swallows us all.

The only difference is so many of you will not be present to see it."

"Why did you open the tea shop?" She pushed her toes through the sheets, feeling the unwinding darkness curling around her legs. "If you don't want to co-mingle with those of us with short lifespans?"

"Ah, I did not say that. I am fascinated by your kind, and the others like you. Topsiders, as you said, must count every second of their existence, and you *live* it so fully. It is not something my sort can ever truly understand, but I do love watching it."

It felt horribly selfish to admit, but she was relieved that she would shuffle off this mortal coil long before them, saving her the heartache of saying goodbye to someone she loved a second time.

"I have a very early delivery being made later this week," they whispered against her neck, threading long fingers through hers. "It's terribly exciting, an addition to my collection. If you would like to be there, perhaps to greet the driver, so that you may see the new acquisition before anyone else . . ."

She chuckled, and the shadows rustled. "I am happy to be your human face so that the delivery driver isn't scared away. You can just say it."

Harper had learned much about the running of the tea shop. They had a limited, set number of seats, and owned a place setting for each seat in triplicate. The delicate pastries came fresh from a local baker every morning, and the ingredients for the savories were from a local farm. The deliveries were made to the back door three times a week, left in the alcove until the truck pulled away and Azathé retrieved them, no signature required.

They hummed, mollified.

"I would be indebted if you would be willing to do so, sweet one. The rest of our deliveries are set up as automatic drops, but the seller for this item is quite insistent on a signature releasing them from responsibility."

"You don't have to be indebted," she laughed into her pillow. "Doing favors for people you care about isn't a hardship. It's hardly a favor, I just need to come to the shop in the morning and sign a clipboard. And if you're going to be indebted to me for that, well, I'm indebted to you for quite a bit more."

Another hum against her neck. Their form had slipped, she could tell. They retained solidity, but the shadows had become malleable and changing. When a tentacle-like tendril around her ankle began to drag up her bare leg, Harper squirmed.

She still wasn't sure how comfortable she was with this arrangement. Despite the fact that she did not form attraction in the same way as most of the people she knew, she was still a sexual being and *desired* sex. But if Azathé derived no pleasure from it . . . despite their assurance that they were not under any sort of supernatural thrall from her latent shadowmancing abilities, she did not want this element of their relationship to be coercive in any way.

"You don't have to do that," she murmured, stiffening slightly when the movement abruptly ceased.

"My apologies, my sweet one. I did not realize the action would be unwelcome."

At that, Harper craned her neck back. "It's not unwelcome. It's *very* welcome. Honestly, the way I've been feeling lately, I would welcome it morning, noon, and night. Twice on Sundays. Don't forget brunch and afternoon snack. But — but I don't want you to feel forced into doing something that's unnatural for you. If it's not pleasurable for you, you shouldn't have to —"

"If giving you pleasure is pleasurable for me, how is it not the same thing, little witch?"

An appendage pushed through her legs, stretching her thighs open until it rested snugly between them, tickling at the front of the panties she still wore, doing exactly what she had fantasized weeks and weeks earlier, that afternoon at the tea shop.

"I seem to remember someone telling me, not all that long ago, that it was pleasurable for them to be used, for their body to be used to give pleasure to another, in any way the other party desired. If I desire you to use me for your pleasure, my Harper, is that not the same? If you pleasure yourself using my form, does some of that pleasure not belong to me?"

The front of the tentacle stroked with more precision than she thought should have been possible for something that hadn't existed only moments earlier. Back and forth, against the dampening gusset, bumping into her clit on every pass. Her shoulders hitched each time it did so, and her hips bucked against the pressure, wanting *more*. Instantly, cold, ghost-like hands fastened around her elbows, holding her in place.

"Sweetling, I do believe you mentioned just earlier the importance of slowing down and not . . . rushing . . . through things."

She trembled as they continued to tease her, stroking against her cotton-covered pussy until the fabric was drenched. She had no complaint when the ruined panties were drawn down her hips, over her legs, and flung away. The arms holding her in place, however, did not give. Harper had a mind to shift her back, opening her legs fully for them, but she was kept on her side, thighs pressed together.

"I believe this is the spot where you are most sensitive, is it not?" Another wriggling finger of smoke pressed between the lips of her sex to circle directly against her clit, making her cry out. "*Very* sensitive, it seems. Show me how you pleasure yourself, sweetling. Use my form and show me."

It was the most erotic experience of her life. Harper tilted her hips, grinding against the fat tentacle that had pushed back between her thighs. Back and forth, she rocked against them, moving her hips as if she were a rodeo star, feeling the textured drag against the lips of her sex. That smaller tendril had circled around her clit, pulsing and pulling, drawing a moan from her throat as if she were a marionette. Her arms were still restrained, and her toes dug into the bedding as she bucked against them. When she did so, the tentacle around her clit tightened like a noose. Not uncomfortable but creating a vacuum of pressure within her that made her eyes roll back every time it pulsed.

The only thing that would make it better was if they were fucking her at the same time, she thought, and no sooner had the consideration formed in her mind, before a thick cock-like protuberance was pressing into the mouth of her cunt. Harper realized there was no end to the forms they could take, of what they could do to her. They could lick her clit and fuck her at the same time, hold her down, take on the knot of a werewolf, the girth of an ogre, the double dick of a dragon, stimulate every single erogenous zone she possessed simultaneously.

"Don't stop," she gasped, an additional shadow tongue licking against the un-hooded swollen pearl, her hips never stopping their motion. "Don't stop. I-I'm going to come. *Fuck*, I'm going to come so hard."

The two wriggling tendrils working at her clit had begun to move in tandem — the pulsing little noose had taken on the same rhythm as the tongue that licked her, the band of pressure that it tightened within her snapping at last. Her moan of pleasure came out on a long whine, whimpering as her body clenched and convulsed, reverberations Azathé surely felt. Her whole body trembled as she came down from her peak, the tentacles slowly retreating.

"Fuck," she laughed, wheezing once she had the ability to see again. "How is it possible that the best sex I've ever had is with someone who has no solid form? Explain to me how that works."

She sunk into her pillows as the darkness swaddled around her.

"Balance in all things, sweet one," they purred, in what Harper was certain was a distinctly smug tone.

Chapter 11

O OTD: Scoop-neck A-line dress with moon embroidered skirt. Mini crinoline. Pentagram harness. Fishnet thigh highs. Platform pumps. Magpie eyeshadow palette and matte lip stain in Midnight. Ribbon choker and HBIC attitude.

Her closet had needed a thorough reorganization, cataloging her shoes and hosiery, determining what needed replacement. If the lack of wanting to care for her wardrobe was a sign her depression was out of control, the desire to shop and repopulate it was certainly a sign it was being well managed, she thought with satisfaction.

Holt had offered her a surprisingly competitive rate of pay, and while it wasn't as much as she would likely be making if she had a full-time office job, it certainly beat typical retail work, with the bonus of being free of office drudgery. He wouldn't be able to have her start until after the solstice holiday, grumbling over the surplus inventory they were currently sitting on, a buying spree completed by his business partner, over which he had no control.

He had appeared on the curb beside her for a second time, simply telling her to get in the car with no further indication of where he might be taking her. Harper felt vague unease, but she obeyed each time, and he had still not cooked her liver. That time, he had driven her to Bridgeton, to The Cat & Crow, the metaphysical and occultist curiosity shop he owned with his former witch. It was located on a small alley, like something out of a movie, the hidden treasure no one knew about except for the local witches.

Holt had rolled his eyes at her declaration. "Yeah, the local witches and all the Halloween store goths. The witch wannabes, the folks just looking for a clever housewarming gift, psychos who collect decapitated doll heads. But oh yeah, we're a well kept secret."

He rolled his eyes again, and Harper was once more possessed with the desire to stab him in the ankle.

"Are all cats jerks, or is it a specific familiar trait?"

"I'm getting rid of all this crap for Christmas," he went on, ignoring her as he gestured to the shelves stretching before them. "That's what all the goths like to buy each other for the holiday — haunted dolls and mortuary equipment. No offense. Bethany is going skiing with her boyfriend, so she won't be here to see me mark it all down. After the first of the year, I take over all the inventory. No more garbage. If you want a set of 18th-century mortuary tools, there's going to be *one* to pick, not seven. We have too much capital invested in product that we can't move. That's when I'll be able to bring you on. Inventory management and pricing research, mostly remote."

Harper laughed. "You're sort of the worst. You know that, right? But that sounds good, I can definitely do that. If nothing else, I'm already familiar with what you carry on the auction and how much stuff sells for. I wonder if there are other shops doing online sales like that? I'm going to search when I get home and follow a few of them."

Holt very nearly purred in response, disappearing down one of the aisles.

She understood his frustration, walking up and down the rows of products. Individually, the items were interesting and unusual, the way they were featured on the weekly auction. But altogether, laid end-to-end on a shelf . . . In the small, space constrained shop, the effect was overwhelming, and the sheer volume of the gimcrack and ephemera made each successive piece seem a little less special. *He's the worst, but he's not wrong. It's just too much stuff.*

Turning a corner, she had found him at the very end of the shop, standing before a wall of ritual candles, her heart tripping over itself in her chest.

"Sabbath candles, chalices, altar tools. I don't have space for a ton of books right now, but if there's ever something you want, I can get it. We'll have more space when I can clear out some of the junk. Ritual herb blends, I'm sure you can guess who my supplier is for that. One-of-a-kind altar cloths. Summoning charms, spell scrolls. We have everything a practicing witch would ever need. And if it is not something I physically have in stock, it is likely something I am able to procure, regardless of how arcane the ingredient or object. We have many suppliers, both on and off the black market. There's no reason for you to not resume your studies, Harper Hollingsworth."

He was rude and blunt and more than just a little bit of a dick. *And possibly a criminal?* Even still, Harper could scarcely remember another time in her life when she had felt as inspired to be a witch. *And when you start working, you can buy new clothes.*

It was with that thought in mind that she undertook the closet project.

She loved the idea of having a reading nook in her house, but her ass loved its couch groove more, and she found the odd-shaped little room sitting empty more often than not, a waste of the minimal real estate her home possessed.

She had wondered endlessly what Pernella had used the space for, arriving eventually on the supposition that it had been her Sabbath spot, used for ritual moon worship and her altar. It seemed as good an explanation as any, Harper thought. She had fallen out of practice with all of her rituals in the past year, and although she was more energized and enthusiastic about resuming her path as she ever had been previously, a devoted altar in her home was still not a good use of the space. Her wardrobe was her point of pride, her barometer of good mental health, and it deserved a place of honor.

She would turn the small room into a walk-in, lined with shelves on two sides and a sturdy rolling rack on the other, taking the pressure off the the minuscule closet her bedroom boasted. DIY home improvement was not her strength, but Harper wasn't inclined to ask for help for this particular project. There were many things that were not her strength, but that didn't mean she ought not attempt them. Perfection was, after all, she reminded herself, unattainable. The brackets had been easy enough to install, and she'd only needed to redo them twice — a triumph, all things considered.

It was in the course of her light construction that she found it. Holt was right. *Fucking know-it-all cat.* Once she'd pulled her armchair and the tottering bookshelves out, Harper had tapped on the walls, looking for studs the way her father always had. She noticed the odd ripple in the wallpaper, almost indistinguishable in the old-fashioned pattern, and when she knocked on that section of the wall, it moved beneath her hand. They hadn't drywalled over the cellar door — they had simply wallpapered over it.

She'd taken her time, feeling all the way down the wall until she could trace the shape of the door. Carefully, using a box cutter, so as not to damage the rest of the wall, she sliced the door free, cutting around the ancient hinges until she was able to pry it open.

You should wait. Call Holt. Or wait for Azathé. You shouldn't go down alone. Rationally, she knew the voice in her head was correct. She had no idea how safe the staircase might be, or what animals may have lurked in the darkness. It would have been smarter and safer to wait until there was someone there with her, lest she fell and was unable to call for help.

She *knew* it would have been smarter to wait, but at that moment, Harper didn't particularly care about being smart. She was being pulled like a magnet, the same witchy core within her that had trembled at Holt's first visit was posi-tively vibrating now. This was *her* great-aunt's library, the same aunt who had been ostracized by her peers. *At least, some of them. The same type who have always ostracized you.* Aunt Pernella had been a powerful and popular witch, at least with a small handful of fellow weirdos, Harper liked to think. The girl from the grocery store parking lot, Lex, was right. There weren't nearly enough weirdos around.

She was relieved to find a banister, worn smooth under her hand as she gripped it tightly. Using her cell phone as a flashlight, Harper rationalized that she could always ask her phone to call for help if she fell. She made it to the bottom of the staircase without incident, her mouth dropping open as she cast her phone's light around the room. The cellar held the exact same dimensions as the cottage above, effectively doubling her living space. Harper could see shelves and shelves of books, an endless amount of books, a long work table, a dark hearth where a cauldron hung . . . And there, in the corner, a lamp. Not a candelabra, nor a stump of a hand-dipped beeswax candle, like she'd been imagining, but the kind of lamp one might've purchased in a department store. *What is wrong with you? Why are you acting as if your grandmother and her sister were indigent medieval villagers? This is the suburbs and it was the 80's!* She swung the flashlight to the wall, finding the light switch easily.

A plump, overstuffed armchair recliner sat beside the lamp, a television tray beside it. The television itself was against the wall — small and old-fashioned, looking as if it weighed three hundred pounds, and Harper grinned. She had been imagining some creepy gingerbread cottage-in-the-forest witch's lair, full of cobwebs and ancient grimoires of dark magic, and possibly the bones of some children in a cage suspended from the ceiling, but it appeared her great aunt used the space to put her feet up, watch television, and eat snacks. *You are literally a witch. Why did you think this was going to be some revisionist fairy tale human nonsense?*

Everything was covered in a thick layer of dust. She pulled her shirt up over her nose and mouth, attempting to breathe in as little as possible, always having suffered from a dust allergy. *If Holt wants to buy any of these books, he's going to hire a cleaner for you first.* Harper tilted her head, approaching the shelves, reading what she could of the spines. The books *were* ancient. It was an impressive collection of spell books through the ages, seemingly on every discipline under the moon. *The perfect place for you to continue your studies.*

She bounced on her toes, face heating, realizing she was very near tears. But, for the first time in nearly two years, it was happiness that overwhelmed her, a sense of purpose finding her at last.

The cleaning crew arrived the very next day, watched over as they worked by a black cat sitting in a high window well. Harper was surprised over the speed in which the familiar acted, requesting that he be granted first refusal of any that she wanted to sell, with the special request of one particular volume from the shelf.

"I'll pay you cash for that one today, as long as I can take it with me."

Locating the book he requested, she examined the cover closely. *When You See Tomorrow Today; Divination For The Modern Sibyl.* Flipping the book open, Harper felt her ocean rock. *From the Library of Willow Brackenbridge.* The knocker at Ladybug's house. Holt's words the very first time he'd shown up on her doorstep — *They're all safe at the Brackenbridge house.* She wasn't sure why tears threatened at the corner of her eyes, reminding herself of her dust allergy as she rubbed them. *His witch was a Brackenbridge.*

"You don't have to pay me anything." Harper was hoping her tone was casual and disaffected, unsure of whether or not she succeeded in her aim. "This didn't belong to my aunt in the first place." Her voice thickened, all hope of unbothered going out the window. *You possess zero chill.* "It's going home to where it belongs."

+ · · + · · · + · · · + · · · + · · · +

OOTD: A-line crepe dress with embroidered bib and white collar. Black tights and knee-high boots, because it's motherfucking spooky season. Smokestack eye palette and suede jacket lip veil. Satin hair ribbon, jeweled ear cuff, and AUNT PERNELLA'S BAT PIN.

"It's been a while since I was last here. But . . . things are going really well. My daughter is thriving at school. She loves her teachers, she loves her classes, she has a million friends. She's a little social butterfly, so she's really in her element every single day. I'm in the process of expanding my business which is thrilling and terrifying." Gentle laughter from around the circle, as the woman pulled a face. "I'm in a new relationship, and . . . I can see him in our forever future. Everything is charmed right now." Abruptly, her eyes filled with tears.

Ava, Harper reminded herself. She made an effort every month to commit to memory the names of the other folks around the circle.

"We're going to be coming up on ten years soon." Her voice broke, and it took several moments before she composed herself enough to continue. "Ten years, which means he'll be gone longer than we were together. And I know wherever he is, he's just thrilled with the way things have turned out. I mean, he's tickled pink watching us, I know it. But I have this weight on my chest, and I feel so guilty. I know it shouldn't. I know we're doing exactly what we are meant to be doing, but sometimes it chokes me."

Harper had learned that her emotional responses were not limited to her own unhappiness. The group met twice a month, and with each person's story — Ava had lost her husband. A moth couple had lost one of their young children. A middle-aged goblin talked about losing her college-age son to addiction, and an exhausted-looking troll had recently lost her mother, after caring for her through a long illness — Harper could barely keep from sobbing.

Even though it probably didn't seem like it on the outside, when she came home with red-rimmed eyes and her head pounding from congestion, she was certain the group was helping. These were her neighbors, people in the community, right here, and they were all going through the same thing. The same endless ocean rocked within each of them, and it made her feel less alone.

Grief is a gift.

She had repeated Holt's words the first time she'd spoken at the group she now attended, after learning that Morgan had been seeing a grief counselor sporadically for the past year.

"Why didn't you tell me?!" she'd gasped in shock when her sister casually mentioned the video call she needed to go in the house and take with her counselor.

Morgan had shrugged. The school had set it up automatically, she explained, long before they moved.

"You weren't living at home, remember? And it wasn't something mom did, the school guidance counselor arranged it. After we moved, I switched to remote appointments with her, and now we only meet once a month. It was weekly before. After. It . . . it really helped having someone to talk to, you know. You should see if there's a support group you could go to."

Harper was furious. She had stomped around the neighborhood that evening, wanting to scream in rage until her throat was raw. The public high school her sister had attended had set up counseling, had ensured she had a support system in place, had made certain she would not drown. The expensive witches' Collegium, fully aware of the circumstances, by contrast, had done nothing, even after it was clear she was struggling — they had shown her the door, had sent her packing to deal with one more blow to her fragile composure, throwing her away as overtly as if she were, in fact, a sack of trash placed outside the minimart's door.

She would not be returning. She might have been undecided up until that point, waffling between not especially wanting to return and still not wanting to disappoint her mother, but now her mind was made up and her conscience clear. She would continue her study alone. She had a veritable library in her basement and Holt could help her fill in the gaps. *And Ladybug is literally just around the corner. Holt said a new coven is coming, and you can join that when it does. You* **are** *a witch.*

The grief support group met twice a month at the community center, and Harper was certain if she had found it a year earlier, she might not have slipped as deeply into that glass-like sea as she had, but there was no more room for what ifs and regrets.

She came home that night with her normal red, puffy eyes, and went straight to the basement. That was where they found her, as they did most evenings when she did not meet them at the tea shop, especially on the nights of those meetings.

"I pulled a card for you today, my sweet one. The Seven of Wands. Holding your ground against adversarial influences. Perseverance. I can think of no card that represents you better, at the moment."

"Flattery will get you everywhere," Harper laughed, opening her arms to be enveloped in their filmy darkness. "That's really good to know, though. I have an appointment tomorrow at my witch doctor's house to find out if it's normal for me to be feeling like I am a werewolf on the cusp of the full moon, or if you have been roofieing me with the tea."

She was mortified over her appointment with Ladybug the following morning, but Harper reminded herself that self-care meant actually taking care of herself, not merely cocooning herself in bed and shutting out the rest of the world. When she woke in the middle of the night, sweat dotting her brow, feeling tangled in her sheets as a fire of desperation burned through her, she reminded herself how lucky she was. Lucky that her mother had sold their childhood home, forcing their move to Cambric Creek. Lucky that her great-aunt had been an eccentric with her own cozy witch's cottage. Lucky that she preferred tea over coffee.

As the shadows wound around her, stretching her legs open and filling her with the thickness they had determined she responded to best, her head dropped back, a breathy moan escaping her. It pleasured them to pleasure her, Aza-thé reminded her constantly. She felt guilty how often she needed to be pleasured lately, but that was the point of her appointment in the morning.

Lucky the shadows had talked to her, and that she had talked back.

+···+···+···+···+···+···+

"Hmmm, I understand. Well, let's see . . . that's probably the ashwagandha. And the ginseng. Oh, and the saffron! And probably the mood enhancers in general . . . Is it becoming a problem? We can scale back on a few of the —"

"Oh, no, no. That's fine. You-you don't need to change anything. It's not a problem." Harper wondered if it was possible to catch fire from embarrassment. Her entire head felt as if she'd just pulled it from an oven, her palms were sweaty, and if the Brackenbridge home had come equipped with a handy dandy hole in the floor, she would have jumped, no questions asked, content to fall directly through the earth.

"I just .. I wanted to make sure it was a possibility and that I wasn't going crazy." *I just wanted to make sure it's normal to be horny all the time.* Harper laughed in embarrassment, but Ladybug only smiled understandingly.

"Increased blood flow, SSRIs, and decreased stress response. Stronger arousal and faster sexual response. I'd be more surprised if you *hadn't* experienced a difference. If you don't have a partner, there's a shop over by the commerce park that sells a huge range of toys. You might need one."

Get a vibrator is the official diagnosis.

Rationally, Harper understood that the chemical imbalances that caused clinical depression also contributed to a lack of sexual response and arousal. It stood to reason, therefore, that the opposite would be true.

The easing of her symptoms had always left her horny, but nothing like this. She was wet day and night. The slightest bit of stimuli against her crotch had her arching, desperate for more. She and her sister had gone to lunch the previous weekend at a brasserie in town, slipping the electronic disc the hostess handed her into the front pocket of her bag. Her cross body bag, that rested on her hip, but at that moment, had been sandwiched between her upper thigh and the counter she leaned on as they waited for their table. When the vibration went off, an indication it was time for them to be seated, Harper almost came right then and there.

If you don't have a partner, there's a toy shop in town to help you get your rocks off.

The problem was she *did* have a partner, one who seemed to enjoy watching her solo play, which only turned her on more.

She hadn't gone to the tea shop that afternoon after lunch with her sister. Instead, she had gone straight home, un-dressing until she was naked from the waist down. When Azathé slipped from the shadows in her bedroom, having come to her house in search of her that evening, they found her in the same position — eyes squeezed shut, teeth gnash-ing, desperate moans pulling from her throat as she held a vibrator to her throbbing clit. She had already come several times since arriving home that day, and felt as if she needed to come several more just to be able to close her eyes and sleep.

Azathé was the most giving shadow partner she could ask for, and was more than willing to assist her . . . but first they wanted to watch her pleasure herself.

"What was it you said about *The Devotion of the Volantines,* witchling? That it was *instructional?* Forgive me, but I find this performance *most* instructional. I hope you'll indulge me."

She had indulged them. They watched her come with the aid of the vibrator, the swirling mass of shadows inches away from her pulsing pussy, a front row seat to her contractions. They watched her straddle her dildo — a strange shaped thing consisting of three fat spheres of descending size, connected on its underside with a thick line of ridges and a curious shaped head. She had bought it years earlier from a shop off campus, and still had no idea what species it was meant to emulate. It didn't matter, for it felt amazing sinking down on each of the spheres, and they had watched that as well, closely examining the way the lips of her sex stretched around the girth, as her breath hitched and her body shook.

When they finally solidified before her to offer her relief, Harper had begged to be taken on her hands and knees, hard and fast and deep, positive the act of actually having sex with someone else would finally cool the fire beneath her skin. The cock they created had the same shape as the dildo, proof that they were an excellent study and that the experiment had, in fact, been quite instructive.

"Do you have any other concerns? Any side effects you want to discuss?"

You mean other than being so horny I feel like a cat girl in heat? She was relieved to hear it was the supplements. Harper understood the science behind it. Granted, she'd never experienced an increase in her libido when she had been on traditional medicine, but the herbal concoction created by the adorably awkward witch had her kitty purring day and night. *As long as it's normal and not a sign you're going to start needing professional intervention in the way of an entire Ketterling team.*

Ladybug was thrilled that Harper was experiencing improvement in her depressive symptoms. "So, uh, obviously I'd like to keep taking it. What do I need to do from here to set up a standing prescription? Or order, whatever you call it?" She followed the other witch, circling the staircase to a rounded parlor, her invoices kept in a small antique secretary desk. As she wrote up the slip, Harper walked around the room. There were photos on all of the walls, all featuring different Brackenbridge witches through the ages, she assumed.

Eyeing an oval portrait of a robust woman with a steel gray updo and a ferocious attitude that Harper was able to discern even through the photograph, she read the inscription on a small brass plaque.

Authricia Brackenbridge

High Crone ~ Cambric Creek Coven

"This is the former high crone! I-I didn't realize you were related. I've heard people talk about her, she sounds amazing." Harper faltered. "Is-is she the witch Holt belonged to?"

Ladybug looked up in surprise, eyes widening. "Holt? Oh, no. No, he belonged to my Aunt Willow. They're just over here . . ."

Rising from her little seat, she led Harper further down the wall, gesturing to a collection of photos. The woman was a beautiful, ethereal blonde, with icy gray eyes and a serene expression. Her fairness made Holt's inhuman spikiness and jet black hair stand out, making him seem even more *other* in the few photos in which he appeared.

The remaining photos were of the same witch, smiling, arm in arm with another woman. Identical features, with darker hair. As Harper moved down the wall, the blonde witch's beautiful platinum hair was replaced with a silk turban, her eyebrows and eyelashes showing the effects of the chemotherapy the head covering hid.

A little girl appeared in a number of the photos, gap-toothed smiles and shining eyes, her mousy brown hair a frizz of loose curls. In one of the photos, the two women sat side-by-side in front of a large cake with candles, the little girl between them. The three of them wore identical silk turbans, and Harper could discern birthday decorations in the background.

"Is this your mother?"

Ladybug nodded, her lips pressed tightly together. "It is," she said after a moment, and Harper wondered if she, too, needed to pull her composure together enough to be able to answer.

It never stops hurting. That's another universal truth. Grief was a bruise on her heart, and it would hurt whenever it was poked. She had a feeling she already knew the answer to the question she asked next.

"Is she –"

"Dead." Another fast nod, lips pressed in a tight line. "They all are. I'm the only one left."

Someday, she would be able to control her emotional responses, perhaps. Someday, but not that day. Harper's eyes overflowed.

"I'm so sorry. My dad died. Last year."

Ladybug nodded again, nodding with a tightly controlled smile, her eyes glossy with tears. "I know. Holt told me. I'm so sorry for your loss. I would ask how you're doing, but I already know."

Choked laughter wrapped in a sob escaped her. "It never stops hurting, does it?"

The other woman's eyes overflowed as she shook her head. "Never. I miss them so much. Sometimes I can hardly breathe around it. It never goes away. But life goes on. You fill your days with other things, you give your heart to new people and hope they'll take care of it. They still walk beside us. They still hold us when we fall. And we'll see them again, eventually."

"Trust," Harper added, once she had swallowed down the sob that she wanted to scream, sucking in a shuddering breath. "Trusting new people to take care of your heart. Trusting yourself to let them love you."

Azathé knew her worries and her fears and her aspirations; stroked her hair when grief occasionally overtook her, remained steadfast and present when depression clouded her mind. *Snap out if it* and *get over it* were never words uttered from their mouth, and the expectation to be nothing more than exactly what she was was intoxicating. *Love* was a completely inadequate word for what she felt for them.

Ladybug smiled, unconcerned over the wet tracks down her cheeks, glasses slipping down her nose. "Trusting them with our hearts is how you know it's real."

＊‥‥＋‥‥＋‥‥＋‥＋‥＋‥＋

OOTD: Leggings, hoodie, it is too early to be alive, wtf

They were beside themselves with excitement.

The delivery had been rescheduled several times, for reasons unbeknownst to Azathé, but now the day was here. Harper had arrived at the teahouse at the ass crack of dawn, as requested, and even though she had determined that she was most definitely *not* an early morning person, she would sooner stay awake for the entire night and day without rest than renege on her promise. She would deny it if anyone claimed to have seen her outfit, but as she stepped into her boots, eyes still blurry with sleep, she couldn't bring herself to care. The little cat hadn't even been there at that hour, and as she came through the door, Azathé gave her an appraising look from the center of the dining room.

"You are the most adorable human I have ever perceived, little witch."

Harper snorted, most unadorably, dropping into a chair and letting her head thunk onto the spirit board table before her. "I'm going to remind you of that fact tonight, when you ride the Ferris Wheel with me." She had been half-joking when she'd said it originally, but Cambric Creek, it turned out, *did* have a Fall Festival, and there *was* a Ferris Wheel.

That morning, they were pacing. Back and forth, across the dining room, from the front door to the kitchen and back again as the minutes ticked by, practically vibrating with their excitement over the impending arrival

"I have just the right spot for it. We didn't even need to move any tables. Just shifted some books and moved to a shelf or two. This is going to be the crown jewel of our collection."

"I'm not so sure about that," Harper deadpanned from her table. She had pulled a tarot deck from the shelf and the three cards before her did not leave her feeling optimistic for her shadowy paramour's new acquisition. "The Two of Cups tells me that you have planned long for this, which is great, but like, no offense? The rest of this spread is high key terrifying. What is this Ten of Swords, Azathé? That's a *nightmare*. Are you bringing a nightmare into the shop? Into our lives?"

They hummed, a static rumble against her, chuffed at her calling it *their* life, together. "Of course not. You're overreacting, sweetling. I thought you said you were giving up on divination."

"I said no such thing, but this Lightning-Struck Tower in the future slot makes me think I need to give up on *town*. Skip out while I have the chance before whatever nightmare you're bringing in here comes to fruition."

They scoffed, a dark ripple against her skin, and she grinned.

Harper wasn't smiling when the movers arrived a short while later. "What the *fuck*?"

"Isn't it beautiful," they crooned, like a proud parent.

"What the **fuck**?! You've got to be kidding me."

Holt's kelpie glared with a crazed expression, looking even more terrifying and mutinous out in the open, now that it was no longer shoved into that cobweb-strewn back hallway of Ladybug's giant house.

"You have no idea how rare this is."

"You have GOT to be kidding me."

"Isn't it majestic?"

"Azathé! That thing is gonna come to life and kill us! No . . . no, wait. It's moved. The head is different. When I first saw this thing, the head was thrown back, like this." She demonstrated for the jubilant shadow, who was paying her panic absolutely no mind. "And now it's turned! It's *snarling*, Azathé! It probably tried to bite someone! Wait, the delivery was postponed, *why*? You need to find out. You bought this from a sketchy, flea-bitten jerk named Holt, right?"

"Names are not traded in these types of transactions, sweetling."

Harper groaned, covering her eyes. "Great, that's just perfect. So he sold this on the black market, and you're the hapless idiot who's going to be eaten in their living room."

"Is Holt not the name of your feline acquaintance?"

"He's a fucking asshole, is what he is," she snarled, feeling the kelpie's eyes on her.

They had learned much about human nature and manipulation, she realized when two curling tentacles hooked around her legs, stroking their way up. "My sweet one," they crooned, a plush velvet press against her, "let me help you ease this agitation."

Harper whimpered at the first stroke to her sex, as her leggings were drawn down. They pressed her flat to the table, ankles gripped in cool hands, rubbing the head of a bulbous tentacle to her always slick folds.

"Wait," she yelped, wanting to do nothing more than close her eyes and let them fuck her into forgetting the murderous horse watching them. "Promise me you're going to contact Holt. Because this thing *is* going to kill someone."

Her breath caught as they pushed into her, her cunt sucking them in, inch by inch, greedy as always.

"And-and promise me you'll ride the Ferris Wheel with me tonight. You don't have to take a form, just . . . stay with me. I want you to see the view."

She wheezed as they bottomed out, the tentacle writhing within her. The kelpie, she was positive, blinked.

"I promise, my sweet one." A silky glide against her neck, cold black satin, like the best-dressed ghost in town. "After all . . . I am happily bound to do your bidding, always."

Harper and Azathé

(and Holt and Ladybug)

~~((and Ilea, unfortunately))~~

will return.

Buckle up, kids.

The season of the witch has arrived.

Hexennacht

Hexennacht.

The Night of Witches, Samhain's calendar twin. It is a night of revelry and dancing and spellwork, of bonfires and sisterhood, culminating in the coven taking to the sky.

Ladybug loved the celebration. It had been her favorite night, once. She remembered spinning before the fire, singing to the moon along with the chorus of sisters around her, elated by the rising euphoria of the ancient circle. Hexennacht was the night she most *felt* like a witch.

It was on another Hexennacht when her fortunes changed.

Cast from the ancient circle, deprived of her place in the sisterhood, dispossessed of belonging. A solitary witch, practicing her craft alone.

But the Fates are fickle, and fortune has changed again.

She never expected to fall in love with the quiet Araneaen upstairs, and could not have foreseen how easily he would spin his web around her heart. The silent, empty days that had stretched before her are now full — in love, no longer alone, her beloved house saved, happier than she can scarcely believe.

All that's missing is a circle of sisters of her own.

In an aging Victorian on a tree-lined street in Oldetowne, the Brackenbridge witches have practiced the craft for generations in a circle unbroken — unbroken still, and now the time has come for the circle to expand.

This year, on the night of witches, a new coven is born, and the most unlikely of their ranks will take her place as a leader.

This high heat, cozy monster romance features a neurodivergent witch FMC and a non-human spider-like MMC and takes place within the Cambric Creek Universe. It is best read as part of the series. Hexennacht is the second volume of The Wheel of the Year and comes after The Mabon Feast.

Pre-order Now

TWO FOR TEA

Extensions – A Steamy Phantom of the Opera Reimagining

C hristine Dyer is trapped.

Trapped in her grief — her father's death has left her alone in the world with no one to turn to for comfort.

Trapped with no future — she can't afford rent *and* tuition, and a roof over her head is more important than her aspirations for the stage . . . but the prospect of taking a minimum wage job and struggling forever hardly feels like a solution to her problems.

Trapped — until she's offered a job that promises heaps of money, the ability to return to school, to pay off the creditors hounding her night and day, the ability to live again, and best of all, she can work from home.

All she has to do is answer the phone. 1-900 - all her problems go away, one happy ending at a time.

Selling sex to strangers from the comfort of her sofa, any hour of the day. No different than any other acting gig.

When she connects with a co-worker on the phone, there's something about his voice, the way he talks to her, the way he comforts her . . . but he's only a voice, and all she has to keep her company in her apartment are her fantasies of him. Soon, Christine can scarcely tell fantasy from reality, and somewhere along the way, she forgets that the first rule of phone sex is to always keep your identity hidden.

Set in mid-1990s NYC, Extensions follows one turbulent summer, when extensions cross and the lines between love and obsession blur.

This loose adaptation of the Phantom of the Opera story is high steam and high tension, coming this December.

Pre-Order Now

ALSO BY C.M. NASCOSTA

Cambric Creek

(Suggested Reading Order)

Morning Glory Milking Farm

A Blue Ribbon Romance

The Mabon Feast (Wheel of the Year)

Sweet Berries

Run, Run Rabbit

Moon Blooded Breeding Clinic

Two For Tea

Hexennacht (Wheel of the Year – Coming Soon)

Girls Weekend

Girls Weekend

Parties

Invitations – (Coming Soon)

Talons & Temptations Historical Monster Romance

How To Marry A Marble Marquis

To Ravish A Rogue

About the Author

C.M. Nascosta is a USA TODAY bestselling author of Monster Romance and a professional procrastinator from Cleveland, Ohio. She's always preferred beasts to boys, the macabre to the milquetoast, the unknown darkness in the shadows to the Chad next door. She lives in a crumbling old Victorian with a scaredy-cat dachshund, where she writes nontraditional romances featuring beastly boys with equal parts heart and heat, and is waiting for the Hallmark Channel to get with the program and start a paranormal lovers series.

+ · · · + · · · + · + · · · + · + · · · +

For exclusive stories, signed paperbacks, bookish merch and more, visit (Updates weekly!):
https://linktr.ee/Monster_Bait

+ · · + · · · + · · + · · + · · · + · · · +

The best way to hear about all things Monster Bait before anyone else is to become a patron:

http://patreon.com/monster_bait

+ · · · + · · · + · · + · · + · · · +

The second best way to stay up-to-date on release news and extras is to follow me on Instagram:

https://www.instagram.com/cmnascosta/

✦ · · · ✦ · · ✦ · · ✦ · · ✦ · · · ✦

The best way to hear about things several days later when I get around to building an email is to join my newsletter: **http://cmnascosta.com/**

Made in the USA
Las Vegas, NV
03 November 2023

80194574R00146